WITHOUT A SHADOW OF DOUBT

Margaret Harris's boss, Jack Stanton, disappears in suspicious circumstances. The police want to track him down, but Margaret believes in him and wants to help him prove his innocence. Meanwhile, Bill Colbourne wants to marry her, but, unsure of her feelings, she can't think of the future until she finds Jack. And, when she does meet with him in Spain, she finally has to admit to Bill that she can't marry him — it's Jack Stanton who she loves.

Books by Teresa Ashby
in the Linford Romance Library:

LOVE ON ICE
FOR THE CHILDREN'S SAKE
THE CALL OF HOME
A ONE-MAN WOMAN
FOOL'S PARADISE
CHERISH THE DREAM

TERESA ASHBY

WITHOUT A SHADOW OF DOUBT

Complete and Unabridged

LINFORD
Leicester

First published in Great Britain in 1997

First Linford Edition
published 2012

British Library CIP Data

Ashby, Teresa.
  Without a shadow of doubt.- -
  (Linford romance library)
  1. Love stories.
  2. Large type books.
  I. Title II. Series
  823.9'2–dc23

  ISBN 978–1–4448–1070–7

Published by
F. A. Thorpe (Publishing)
Anstey, Leicestershire
Set by Words & Graphics Ltd.
Anstey, Leicestershire
Printed and bound in Great Britain by
T. J. International Ltd., Padstow, Cornwall

This book is printed on acid-free paper

A Jealous Quarrel

Margaret Harris drove automatically along the narrow, twisting country lanes. It had been her choice to take the back roads from Stanley-Under-Lyme to the motorway. She needed time to adjust to the hustle and bustle of Stanford and her demanding job at Stanton Import-Export after the peace and quiet of the weekend.

The early morning sun shone through the trees, dappling the road ahead with mellow light. It was going to be a beautiful day, she thought a little wistfully.

She slowed down, seeing a magpie at the edge of the road. It looked up, saw the car coming and rose into the air, shrieking angrily.

'Morning, Captain Jack.' She didn't really believe lone magpies were harbingers of ill luck, but old habits die hard.

She rounded a tight bend and had to

brake sharply as she caught up with a tractor towing a trailer.

As soon as he realised he was being followed, the driver leaned out of his cab and waved, signalling that he'd be pulling in soon.

She waved back. He looked familiar. She probably knew him through Bill Colbourne.

She slowed down even more, allowing the tractor to pull ahead. Bill . . . did she want to marry him or not?

Most people, including her parents and younger brother and sister, seemed to expect it. Bill certainly did — but she wasn't sure, particularly after this weekend.

It had started off well enough . . .

Bill had come round to her parents' house shortly after she'd arrived on Friday evening. His dark eyes were glittering as he gave her a quick kiss and a hug.

'Right, come on,' he'd said without preamble, grabbing her hand and all but dragging her from the kitchen. 'It's

2

really taking shape!' he exclaimed as he opened the door of his Land-Rover and waited impatiently for her to climb in.

'I suppose you mean the museum?'

'The Stanley-Under-Lyme Folk Museum.' His voice was proud. 'You should see some of the machinery I picked up in Scotland. It still had my grandfather's name on it.'

He started the engine and they set off with a jerk. Margaret had never seen him so full of enthusiasm.

'How about your father?' she asked. 'I thought he wanted to knock the old place down?'

'He's starting to come round. In fact, I think he's actually quite taken with the idea now.'

He was behaving like an overgrown schoolboy and Margaret found she was getting swept along by the tide of his enthusiasm.

He stopped the Land-Rover in the yard of Colbourne Agricultural Machinery and Engineering, which Bill and his father ran together.

'Imagine.' He gazed through the windscreen. 'My great-grandfather started off with a smithy in that very building. I couldn't let Dad tear it down to make room for his new sheds.'

'So you nagged, pleaded and persuaded until he agreed to build his sheds over there instead.' Margaret laughed as she got out of the Land-Rover. The new buildings stood behind a glade of trees, all concrete and plastic in complete contrast to the old.

That had been eighteen months ago. Now Bill's folk museum was finally taking shape in the old smithy.

'I've been all over the country for old tools and farm machinery. You'd be surprised how much I've found. Come on, I'll show you round.'

He grabbed her hand to pull her along in his eagerness.

Last time she'd been here, it had been dark and cobwebby with a few unrecognisable rusty tools scattered about. She couldn't believe how much it had changed.

'You've been working hard!'

'I've got the old bellows working.' He went over to the huge fireplace. 'I intend to give demonstrations — actually have a fire burning — and show people how it used to be done.'

'All in period costume, of course,' she smiled.

'Absolutely!' He grinned back at her. 'Come on, there's more.'

He led her round and she found, to her surprise, that she was thoroughly enjoying herself. Was it the exhibits or Bill's enthusiasm that brought the past to life before her eyes?

'I've even got the backing of the local council,' he was saying. 'I'll be ready to open to the public in a couple of weeks.'

'You've done wonders! And I'm so pleased that your father is in favour of it now. I must admit, I never thought he'd come round.'

'Neither did I. He kept going on about how it was all a waste of time and money.' Bill sounded rueful. 'Now, I think he's quite pleased — but he'd never let on! I just catch him looking at some of the old stuff in here with a gleam in his eye. Brings back memories, I suppose.'

Later, as they sat in the garden at the Royal Oak, Margaret managed to turn the conversation from the past to the present.

'How's the business going now? Are things picking up?'

Bill nodded. 'At last. We did go through a sticky patch, as you know. Like everybody else, farmers weren't buying any new equipment. They were even skimping on the servicing. But Dad took advantage of the lull to build the new sheds. He doesn't mind investing in the future and he never doubted things would improve. And they have, thankfully.'

'I'm glad to hear it.'

'We can thank your father for a lot of it. He's done a great deal to help people in the area. He's the best bank manager we've ever had round here. He knows the people, knows what will — and what won't — work. In fact, I'm surprised the bank lets him stay here. I'd have thought he'd be promoted.'

'Oh, it's not that he hasn't been given the chance.' Margaret laughed. 'More than once, in fact. But he likes it here, refuses to budge. He's not very popular at head office because of it!'

'Well, a lot of people are grateful to him,' Bill assured her. 'The Colbournes included.'

* * *

The tractor in front pulled off the road into a farm gateway to let Margaret pass and she put her foot down, giving the driver a cheery wave and an appreciative toot on her horn as she sped past.

Once past, with a clear road ahead, she found her thoughts returning to the weekend.

Seeing Bill's new venture taking shape had been fun — but then the

7

weekend had begun to deteriorate.

It had all started when Bill had turned the conversation round to them. If only he hadn't got so serious! But once he got an idea in his head, he was like a dog with a bone . . .

She enjoyed sharing his enthusiasms and his triumphs and he always made her laugh, but the minute he became serious, she started to feel trapped.

'Do you have to carry on working in Stanford?' he'd asked her.

Her heart sank. She knew what was coming next.

'Why don't you come home? Where you belong. You could get a job . . . you could work for me . . . '

'I don't want to work for you. I've already got a job — a good one I enjoy.'

'Oh, the independence thing again.' He waved his hand dismissively. 'But you've done that now, haven't you?'

She stared at him in amazement for a moment.

'You're just a male chauvinist!' she

told him sternly.

'Well — ' He hesitated, uncomfortable because she was glaring crossly at him. 'I'm sorry if that's how it sounds, but I can't help it. You know how I feel about you. If you're really set against working for me, then . . . will you marry me?'

She took a long, deep breath.

'That's about the most romantic proposal a girl . . . '

Before she could say another word, he'd taken her in his arms and kissed her.

It would have been so easy to melt in his arms, to give herself over entirely to his kiss . . .

When they broke apart, he looked down at her, triumph shining in his dark eyes. With a stern look, she pressed her hand to his chest and pushed him gently but firmly away.

'Don't say you didn't enjoy it.' His voice was husky.

'I wasn't going to.' She couldn't help smiling. 'You know how I feel about you. I like you. I like being with you. I even like kissing you! But I'm not ready for marriage — or any serious commitment — yet.'

His face took on a sulky expression, making him look just like a schoolboy.

'So I just have to hang around until you're ready?' he said huffily.

'I didn't mean it to sound like that,' she protested.

'Well, it did,' he retorted, peeved.

'I'm sorry,' she said placatingly, but after that they didn't exchange two words until they'd left the pub and Bill parked the Land-Rover on a hill overlooking the town.

The atmosphere was so thick between them, Margaret felt she could have cut it with a knife.

'This job of yours — ' Bill broke the silence at last. ' — that you enjoy so much. I suppose it has a lot to do with Jack Stanton?'

'Of course it has a lot to do with Jack Stanton.' Margaret was tired, her voice weary. 'He's my employer. And a good one, too. I'll always be grateful that he gave me the chance to prove myself. And, please, don't start about him and me having something going. He's my boss. That's all there is to it. Honestly.'

Bill deliberately ignored her plea.

'I've met him, remember. He's a real operator. He's ... well, he's got a reputation. A high flier.'

'And what's wrong with that?'

He shifted uncomfortably in the driving seat.

'Well, I'm just a simple country lad . . .'

'You?' she interrupted him. 'A simple country lad! That'll be the day!'

He shrugged. 'Compared with Jack Stanton, I am. And there's you, jetting off abroad, sharing hotels with him . . .'

'Hotels, yes,' she agreed. '*Not* hotel rooms!'

'I should hope not! My point is — you don't have to do it. And I don't have to hang around here waiting for you to come home. There are plenty of other girls who would appreciate — '

'Then maybe you should find one!' she broke in.

11

From there things had simply gone from bad to worse.

Now Margaret felt guilty, on top of everything else, for having treated him so badly. But if only he wouldn't try to take control of her life . . .

She came to the main road and joined the morning traffic, beginning to build up now, she noted. She'd better pay more attention to her driving . . .

Instead her thoughts turned towards Jack Stanton . . . Dynamic and energetic, he was still just in his mid-thirties, having taken over the company when his father died suddenly of a heart attack.

Working with him was demanding. It stretched her to her limits — and she enjoyed every minute of it. It was so different from the quiet country life she'd have with Bill . . .

He was right about Jack having a reputation. For ambition . . . hard work . . . determination . . . But what was wrong with that?

Sometimes Margaret wondered if she

was a little bit in love with Jack. Then she'd dismiss the fancy as ridiculous. Jack had never given her any reason to think he saw her as anything but a valued employee.

Oh, they often had meals together and she frequently accompanied him abroad. But it was always strictly business.

She frowned. Recently Jack had changed. He'd been looking strained. And his tan had started to fade, leaving him looking wan and tired. Still, no wonder. Stanton Import-Export, just like Colbourne Farm Machinery and Engineering, had suffered from the recession, and Jack had stretched himself beyond reasonable limits to keep the company going, even bringing two new accountants on to the board from a Middle Eastern bank.

Although she had no say in such matters, Margaret had tried to warn him against getting too closely involved with them. She felt he was getting into waters that had very big financial sharks.

'We have to move with the times,

Margaret,' he'd told her when she'd tried to talk to him. 'Gone are the days when we could finance our own plans. If you want to think big — and it's the only way these days — you have to move in with the big boys.'

With trade barriers coming down all across Europe, Jack had turned his eye towards the new Russia. He saw it as a big potential market, but a great deal of money was needed to back his ambitious plans.

'Don't worry,' he'd told her with his ready grin. 'With these powerful people behind us, we'll really go places.'

Margaret cruised along the motorway. It seemed strange not to be heading for the head office of Stanton Import-Export. Today she was going to the other side of town, where Jack had set up a meeting at a large country house hotel. They had been working together on the project for a month and today was the day contracts would be signed. He would be waiting for her . . .

Where's Jack?

As she drove into the carpark at the hotel, Margaret realised Jack's car wasn't there.

'Good morning, Miss Harris.' The young man on reception smiled in welcome.

'Good morning.' She beamed back brightly. 'When Mr Stanton arrives, would you please tell him I'm in the lounge?'

'Certainly. Shall I have coffee sent through?'

'Yes, please.'

The coffee arrived, and time passed. Margaret began to grow anxious. Jack should have been here by now. He was never late for a meeting and the clients were due to arrive at any moment.

She went over to the window and looked out at the carpark. There was still no sign of his car.

She returned to the reception desk.

'Any word from Mr Stanton?' she asked hopefully.

'I'm afraid not, Miss Harris.'

'How odd,' she was musing as the revolving door began to move and she turned to it with no little relief. But it wasn't Jack. With a sinking heart, Margaret realised the clients had arrived.

After polite greetings, she led the three men through to the lounge.

'I won't keep you a moment,' she said, once they were seated. 'I'll order coffee. Or would you prefer something else?'

'Coffee would be fine, thank you, Miss Harris,' they murmured politely.

She hurried back to reception. She was very anxious now. What on earth could have delayed Jack? She'd never known him keep important clients waiting. It wasn't like him at all.

After she'd ordered coffee, she took out her mobile phone and called the office.

'Jack hasn't been in at all today,' his secretary told her. 'He said on Friday he'd be going straight to the hotel to meet you. It's not like him to be late, is it?'

Margaret thanked her and hung up, then punched in Jack's mobile number. No answer. Then she tried his home number. His answering machine cut in.

She left a message asking him to call her, then hung up and called his mother. Perhaps he had spent the weekend with her?

'Jack? No, I haven't seen him. Why, is something wrong?'

Mrs Stanton sounded worried and Margaret was quick to reassure her.

'Not at all. He's probably on his way here right now.'

'He may be held up in traffic,' Mrs Stanton suggested.

'Yes, I'm sure that's it,' Margaret said. 'I'm sorry to have bothered you.'

She took a deep breath before returning to the hotel lounge.

'I'm sorry to keep you waiting.' She

managed to sound cheerful. 'I'm afraid Mr Stanton has been unavoidably delayed — but I'm sure he'll be here just as soon as he can.'

'I hope he's not going to be long.' One of the men looked pointedly at his watch. 'I've another meeting at twelve.'

'Perhaps we could go over the contract while we wait?' she suggested. 'Mr Stanton has suggested one or two minor alterations I know he meant to discuss with you this morning.'

Looking at their disapproving faces, she wished that Jack would breeze in and take over, but determinedly pushed the feeling aside to put across the points she knew he wanted to make.

She took as long as possible but, finally, she was left with very little more to say.

There was an awkward silence. The men looked at each other. One spoke.

'Look, Miss Harris, we were meant to meet here at nine. It's now eleven and he's a no-show. Exactly where is Jack Stanton?'

Margaret felt her heart sink. It was quite obvious that Jack wasn't coming and she felt anxious and angry at the same time. Where was he?

She thought quickly.

'I'm very sorry but I can only imagine he has been unavoidably delayed and for some reason can't contact us via his mobile phone. Would you consider giving us an extra twenty-four hours? You could sign now and I'll get Mr Stanton's signature by this time tomorrow,' she suggested hopefully.

The men stood up, their faces grim.

'I'm afraid that's just not good enough, Miss Harris.'

'I'm sorry.' She fought to keep her voice level. 'It's the best I can offer in the circumstances. But won't you reconsider? We've worked hard to put this together — please don't let's lose it all now.'

They all glanced at each other, and she saw one nod faintly.

'All right. You have twenty-four

hours. Get this to my office by eleven o'clock tomorrow — with Jack Stanton's signature on it — and I'll sign.'

She suppressed a sigh of relief.

'Thank you. I can only say again how very sorry I am about all this.'

She waited until they'd gone, then drove quickly through town to the office. All during the journey she was looking hopefully for Jack's car, but she was disappointed.

★ ★ ★

Louise Carter, Jack's secretary, was working at her computer as Margaret came in. She looked up, smiling.

'Where's Jack? I've got a pile of phone messages for him.'

Margaret sighed. 'I was hoping he'd be here.'

'I haven't seen hide nor hair of him,' Louise replied. 'He didn't turn up for the meeting then?'

'No. And the clients weren't at all happy about it, I can tell you! What on earth's he playing at?'

Louise frowned thoughtfully. 'It's not like him to miss any appointment, let alone one as important as this one was. Do you think something's happened to him?'

'I really don't know. I've tried calling his mobile and his home number, and his mother's — but no joy.' Margaret shook her head. 'I don't know where else to look.'

The door opened and Denis Brown walked in, a sheaf of papers in his hand. Margaret and Denis had both applied for the job as Jack's assistant and he hadn't been best pleased when she'd been chosen over him.

'Hello, Margaret,' he said coolly. 'So — where's the big man?'

'Still not turned up,' Louise answered. 'We're getting worried about him.'

Denis frowned. 'That's not like him.'

'That's what I said,' Margaret agreed. 'I've never known Jack go off without a word before. I don't suppose you have any idea where he might be?' she asked, hope in her voice.

Denis thought for a moment.

'You've tried his mobile? And his home? And his mother's?'

Margaret nodded and Denis looked defeated.

'Then I'm no more help — I can't think where else he might be.' He looked at Margaret. 'What happened at the meeting?'

'I managed to get them to give us another twenty-four hours. It was the best I could do. I just hope Jack turns up soon.'

Denis was still trying to think of possible explanations.

'If he'd broken down somewhere, he'd have phoned. Unless . . . there was an accident.'

'We'd have heard if there was, surely?' Louise protested.

'I'm sure we would,' Denis reassured her. 'Who saw him last?'

'I left early on Friday,' Margaret recalled. 'I was going to my parents' in Stanley-Under-Lyme.'

'And I left just on five,' Denis added. 'I had a squash game.'

'So it must have been me,' Louise decided. 'You know how he is for getting things cleared up before the weekend. He was still here when I left about half-past five.'

They all frowned, deep in thought.

'Did he seem all right to you?' Margaret asked.

'Well, he's been a bit . . . odd lately. You must have noticed. Sort of . . . preoccupied I suppose . . . But yes, yes, he seemed all right.'

'All we can do is wait.' Denis shrugged. 'Or call the police?' he added doubtfully.

'It's a bit early for that,' Margaret decided. 'Anyway, don't you have to be missing for more than a few hours before the police can do anything? We'll just have to wait and keep our fingers crossed.'

★ ★ ★

For the rest of the day, Margaret kept hoping Jack would turn up. She called his mobile and home numbers again and again, with no reply. She even had the office messenger pop round on his motorbike to Jack's flat, to see if there was any sign of him.

At the back of her mind was the memory that Jack's father had been struck down with a heart attack. And Jack had been under a great deal of strain lately . . .

The messenger reported back that the flat seemed empty and Jack's car wasn't in its parking space.

At five o'clock everyone packed up to leave. Word had got round about Jack's mysterious disappearance and speculation was rife.

Margaret tried to play it down, even suggesting that he might have been delayed on an unexpected business trip. Anything, she thought, to stop the gossip.

'I'm going to stay on for a while,' she told Louise when she looked in to her office to say goodnight. 'Would you lock up as you leave?'

'Sure you'll be all right? I can stay on for a bit if it would help?' Louise offered.

'I'm all right.' Margaret smiled. 'It's Jack I'm worried about.'

Louise turned in the doorway. 'Try not to. He's a big boy! I doubt if anything awful has happened. He'll probably turn up tomorrow morning and wonder what all the fuss has been about.'

'I hope so.'

Margaret went on working long after Louise had left the building. With Jack absent, there was a lot more work for her. All she could do was try to keep things ticking over until he came back.

She was so immersed in her work that the sudden noise made her jump.

She held her breath, listening hard.

Someone was moving about downstairs!

Jumping to her feet, she rushed out to the landing and looked over the banister rail.

'Jack? Jack, is that you?'

'Sorry, Miss Harris. I saw the lights on and thought I'd better check it out.' The security guard who patrolled several businesses in the area looked up at her from the stairwell. 'It's not often I see anyone working here on a Monday night.'

'Oh, I see. Well, thanks for checking. I'm just about to leave now anyway.'

'All right, m'dear.' He smiled. 'I'll be off now then.'

Back in her office, Margaret shut down her computer and set the fax machine to transmit several pages of material. Then she took some files into Jack's office to put them away.

Automatically she checked that everything was locked — but to her surprise Jack's small private cabinet swung open when she touched it.

Quickly she checked. Yes — there were a couple of files missing!

She frowned and checked again. What was going on?

She turned to his desk where she had left the contract. She couldn't leave that lying around all night. She would put it in the safe. That was where Jack normally kept important papers as well as a significant amount of cash.

She opened up the safe — and gasped in amazement. It was almost empty. All the money was gone — and so were some of the papers!

No-one in the office could have taken anything. Only she and Jack knew the combination . . .

She tried Jack's phone numbers again before she left the office, with the same results as before. She was beginning to feel quite sick with worry. What had happened to him?

There must be a simple explanation, she told herself firmly. But no matter how many times she added it up in her mind, it didn't make sense. Jack, cash and files missing. Why?

* * *

Back home in her own flat she checked her answering machine as soon as she got in. The light was winking, indicating at least one message. Maybe Jack had called?

She pressed the replay button and listened intently.

'Hello! It's Judith. Badminton — Thursday — eight pm. Don't forget! See you.'

The next message was simply a click where the caller had hung up. That wasn't unusual. A lot of people didn't like speaking to a machine.

The next one was Judith again.

'Er . . . hi, it's me again. Badminton's off, I'm afraid. I've got a big date for Thursday. You don't mind, do you, Mags? Call me.'

There were five more messages, each one just a click where the caller had hung up. She stared at the machine and bit her lip. She wouldn't normally expect to have so many dead calls waiting for her.

She fixed herself a sandwich and sat down in front of the television to eat, even though she wasn't at all hungry.

There was more than fatigue behind her lack of appetite, she thought as she nibbled at the sandwich. She was worried about Jack — but was there more to her anxiety than just friendly concern?

She yawned. It had been a long day. She would just catch up on the TV news, then a quick bath and off to bed.

The next moment, she was sound asleep in the chair . . .

The noise, part of a dream, was insistent and annoying. A bell was ringing . . . alarm bell . . . telephone . . .

She jerked awake and sat up. She had a stiff neck from her position in the chair and her vision was blurred. The television screen was murmuring away to itself.

It took her a moment to get her bearings, then all the worry came flooding back.

The bell rang again and she hurried to answer it, staggering a little, still feeling dizzy from sleep. Who on earth could it be in the middle of the night?

She slipped the security chain into place before opening the door a crack and peering out.

'Jack!'

She fumbled with the chain to open the door fully. She'd never been so pleased to see anyone in her life — even if he did look dreadful. He had at least a day's growth of stubble on his chin and he looked as if he hadn't slept for ages. His hair was ruffled and his blue eyes were pink-rimmed and bloodshot.

She was so relieved to see him, it was all she could do not to hug him.

Then relief turned to anger.

'Have you any idea of the trouble you've caused?' she demanded as she ushered him in. 'It was so embarrassing when you didn't turn up for that meeting. I was left twittering like an idiot — and the clients were furious! How could you do that?' she ranted on. 'The office has been in uproar all day! And now you turn up here in the middle of the night . . .'

She broke off and ran her hand

through her hair. Ridiculously, she felt like bursting into tears.

He reached out to her, gripping her arms. His hold was firm, steadying and reassuring.

'I'm sorry for putting you through all that.' He gazed deep into her eyes as he spoke. 'I've been trying to reach you.'

'Why didn't you call the office? Or my mobile?'

'I didn't want to risk anyone hearing. When I called here all I got was that blasted answering machine!'

'I know the feeling.' She managed a smile at last. 'I've been trying to call you, too.'

'Things are probably going to get worse tomorrow,' he went on, his tone urgent. 'You'll be getting a visit from the police. They'll probably have a warrant to search the office. And if they don't yet, they soon will have.'

'Why? What on earth's happening? Are you in trouble? What have you done?'

He shook his head, silencing her flow of questions.

'There isn't time,' he said. 'I'm leaving the country in — ' He checked his watch. 'In about four hours from now. I just wanted to see you before I leave, to tell you that everything will be all right — eventually. I promise you that.'

For a moment, she wondered if this was part of a nightmare. Would she wake up in a few seconds? But there was nothing dreamlike about Jack's presence.

'Why me?' she whispered.

'Because you're the only person I can trust. The other board members — ' He broke off, looking bitter. 'You do trust me, don't you, Margaret?'

She was about to reply that of course she did, but he didn't give her the chance.

'You must!' he burst out. 'Whatever happens, you've got to trust me!'

'Have you come here at this time of night just to tell me that?' she asked incredulously, beginning to shiver.

'No, there's something else,' he admitted.

He reached into his inside jacket pocket and withdrew a brown envelope.

'Will you keep this safe for me? Until I come back, or . . . '

He looked around her sitting room. There was something about his expression that frightened her. He looked cornered.

'Yes, it'll be safe here,' he murmured, then turned back to look at her. 'Don't tell anyone about it, not even the police. And . . . and don't tell them I was here. Apart from that, you must co-operate with them as best you can. The last thing I want is for you to get into trouble over this.'

'But . . . '

'Please. Please, just trust me?'

He gave her the envelope and she stared at it.

'What is it?'

'It's better that you don't know,' he said mysteriously. 'I've never asked so much of you before . . . I've never needed anyone so much before. Please, Margaret . . . I wouldn't put you in this position unless it was absolutely necessary. I'm not happy about doing it, but I have no choice. I need you . . . ' he repeated.

'Can't you tell me what it's all about?' she pleaded.

'The less you know the better.' He looked at his watch again. 'I'll have to go.'

'Take care.' She didn't know what else to say.

She was shivering. The night had turned suddenly ice cold.

He looked at her for a long time, then leaned forward and softly kissed her cheek. His lips were as light and swift as a butterfly's wings.

She touched her face, but before she could say anything, he rushed out of the flat, leaving the door to swing shut behind him.

She stared uncomprehendingly at the closed door, listening to the lift whirring softly as it took him downstairs and away.

Thank Goodness For Bill

The following morning, Margaret was in the shower when she heard the telephone. She dashed to answer it, half expecting it to be Jack.

'Margaret?' Bill Colbourne sounded either excited or upset, she couldn't tell which. 'I was about to hang up! What took you so long?'

'I was in the shower,' she explained. 'What's so urgent? Has something happened?'

'I was hoping you'd tell me. Haven't you heard the news? It's even on breakfast television.'

'What is?' Margaret was getting exasperated. The last thing she needed now was Bill talking in riddles.

'Jack Stanton! He's in some kind of trouble.'

'Oh, Jack . . . ' she whispered.

The envelope he'd given her the

night before was still on the table where she'd left it. She stared at it. What was in it? And what could be so important . . . ?

'Margaret, are you still there?'

For a moment she was tempted to confide in Bill, tell him all about Jack coming to the flat . . .

'What's he up to? Do you know?' Bill's voice interrupted her thoughts. 'The police are pulling your office apart!'

'They're what?'

'It's only speculation at the moment, of course, but the DTI are involved. It looks like your Jack has been exporting things to places he shouldn't.'

'Don't be ridiculous.' Margaret felt colour flare to her face as she leapt to Jack's defence. 'I've worked with Jack long enough to know he wouldn't do anything illegal.'

'I expected you to stick up for him.' Bill sounded a little sour and she had the awful feeling that he was pleased about all this.

'I'll have to go,' she said. 'I'm sorry, but if what you say is true I really should be getting to the office.'

'Margaret . . .'

'Goodbye, Bill. I'll speak to you later.'

She hung up, aware that her heart was drumming.

'This isn't happening,' she said to herself, as she turned on the television. Bill must have made a mistake . . .

However, when the local news bulletin came on, showing the familiar building of Stanton Import-Export, she knew it was true. There was a police barrier in front of the building, and behind it she could see people going in and out of the office carrying boxes of files and papers and even the computers.

As she watched with mounting disbelief, the telephone rang again.

'Margaret?' She recognised the slightly shaky voice of Jack's mother. 'What's happening? Why are the police taking everything out of Jack's office?'

'I really don't know,' Margaret replied truthfully. 'I've only just seen the news myself.'

'And why is the Department of Trade and Industry involved? Stanton's has always had a good relationship with them. I know Jack relied on you — surely you must know something?'

'Please, try not to worry, Mrs Stanton.' Margaret sounded a lot calmer than she felt. 'I'm sure this has all been a dreadful mistake.'

'And where's Jack?' Barbara Stanton was clearly near to tears. 'I can't reach him.'

'I don't know the answer to that either, I'm afraid. I know it's easier said than done, but please try not to worry, Mrs Stanton.'

What had Jack said to her last night? Things would probably get worse and the police would want to speak to her?

What for? She hadn't done anything.

'Look, I'll try to find out what's happening. And, as soon as I know anything, I'll call round,' she promised.

'Would you, dear? Oh, thank you.'

As soon as she had finished speaking to Mrs Stanton, Margaret picked up the envelope. Should she open it?

'Oh, Jack.' She sighed, biting her lip. 'What have you done?'

But, as she dressed, the envelope was still sealed. Even if it was important, she had given Jack her word . . .

Whatever it was, she shouldn't leave it lying about. She looked around. Where was a safe place? Her eye fell on the cushion in the armchair. Quickly she unzipped the cover and slid the envelope inside, then zipped it up and put it back in place. She looked at it critically. Yes, it looked perfectly normal.

With a last look around her flat, she left for the office.

* * *

Two policemen were standing at the entrance to the car park. Margaret slowed and wound down her window to speak to them.

'Can you let me through? I work here.'

'Sorry, miss.' One of the officers bent down to answer her. 'No-one can go in.'

'I have to know what's happening,' she insisted. 'Isn't there someone here I can speak to?'

She caught sight of the night security man, hovering by the gate.

'I'm sorry, m'dear,' he said, approaching. 'I had to let them in. They had a warrant.'

He turned to the policeman. 'This is Miss Harris — Mr Stanton's personal assistant. I think you should tell someone she's here.'

The policeman straightened up, turned his back and spoke into his radio. After a few minutes, he came back to her.

'Someone's coming to see you, miss. Just wait here, please.'

Margaret sat impatiently drumming her fingers on the steering wheel. How dare they stop her going into her own office!

A man in overalls came out of the

building carrying a computer. He bumped it against the wall and Margaret leapt from her car.

'For goodness sake be careful!' she cried. 'That's expensive equipment! Don't damage it!'

'You must be Margaret Harris,' a deep voice said.

She swung round. The man who had spoken was tall and broad and looked every inch a policeman.

'Who are you? Are you going to tell me what's going on? How dare you take all this equipment?'

He smiled down at her and took his identity card from his pocket.

'I'm Detective Chief Inspector Ian Travers, Stanford CID. This is Mr Derek Moss from the DTI and my colleague, Detective Sergeant Hilary Walker. Would you mind coming with us, please? One of my officers will park your car.'

'Thank you.'

She handed over her keys, relieved that someone was prepared to talk to her. But, as she followed Inspector Travers across the car park, her legs felt like jelly.

They went straight to her office. All her filing cabinets and computer had been removed.

'Where . . . ?' she began.

'There's nothing to worry about, Miss Harris. We just want to ask you a few questions. Please sit down.'

Margaret took a seat. The detective sergeant stood by the window and the man from the DTI sat on a chair in the corner. Inspector Travers sat on the edge of the desk and looked down at her.

Margaret scolded herself. Why was she so apprehensive? She hadn't done anything wrong. She didn't even know what all this was about!

'What can I do for you?' Her mouth felt dry, but she was determined to appear calm.

'We'd like to know where Jack Stanton is,' Inspector Travers said.

'So would I!' There could be no

doubt she was telling the truth. 'I was hoping you'd tell me!'

Ian Travers smiled and she began to relax a little.

'Don't look so worried, Miss Harris,' he said. 'I'm sure we'll get to the bottom of this sooner or later.'

'Get to the bottom of *what*? I do wish you'd tell me what this is all about.'

'Do you know anything about Stanton's exports to South America, via the Middle East?'

She frowned. 'There's nothing to know. We don't export to South America. And if we did, we would export direct.'

'You know that it's illegal to export — er, certain things — without a licence?'

'Jack would never . . . ' Margaret's head began to spin. After lying awake half the night worrying, she was finding it hard to think straight.

'We found Jack Stanton's car last night,' DCI Travers was saying. 'Were you aware it had been reported stolen?'

'No. But that explains why we couldn't get through to his car phone.'

'It's been completely stripped, Miss Harris. Obviously whoever took it was looking for something. Have you any idea what that might be?'

'No!' Margaret remembered the package under the cushion in her flat and felt ill. 'Look, am I under suspicion? If I am, I'd like to speak to a lawyer.'

Inspector Ian Travers stared at her, his blue eyes as cold as ice. She shivered.

'Not to worry, Miss Harris.' He smiled suddenly, throwing her off guard. 'But we would like you to open the safe for us.'

Margaret walked with him to Jack's office.

'You seem very nervous,' he remarked.

She glanced at him and he smiled. 'It wasn't meant as a criticism, or even a suggestion, just an observation.'

'Well, wouldn't you be? I haven't a clue what's going on and, to be honest, I'm scared.'

'He really didn't confide in you at all?' he asked.

'Look, I know Jack as well as anyone,' she told him as he pushed open Jack's office door. 'He wouldn't break the law. He values his reputation too much for that.'

'What about his new partners?'

Her lips tightened. 'I can't speak for them,' she told him curtly.

'What if he found out they weren't what they seemed? What if he discovered they were using his good name as a cover?'

She turned horrified eyes on him.

'Is that what you think has happened?'

The inspector spread his hands. 'I'm keeping an open mind, Miss Harris. But, if that were the case, what do you think Jack Stanton would do?'

Margaret thought for a moment.

'He'd sort it out,' she whispered.

'If that's the case, then his life could be in danger. On the other hand, if he's just a crook, he'll be living it up on some tropical beach!'

Incensed, Margaret walked over to the safe and opened it.

'Is anything missing?' the policeman asked behind her.

'I don't know,' she said. 'Jack kept cash in here. That's gone. As for papers . . . I'm not sure.'

But there *was* something else! Jack had also kept his computer's floppy disks in the safe! The ones where he stored confidential information. Now they'd gone. Were they in the envelope back at her flat?

'We've been following him for weeks,' the inspector was saying. 'Last night he managed to give my boys the slip and vanished. Are you sure you don't know where he is?'

'No.' What else could she say?

'Any idea why he chose last night to disappear?'

Margaret closed her eyes, shaking her head. Would they believe she knew nothing?

The inspector sighed.

'Are you aware that Jack Stanton's

home has been searched? And his car? We're not dealing with an ordinary burglary, Miss Harris. This has been done by professionals. Why? What are they looking for?'

She opened her eyes and stared at him.

'You're the policeman,' she said quietly. 'You tell me.'

He shook his head.

'We've almost finished here. I'll be in touch again, Miss Harris. If you hear from Jack Stanton . . .

'I understand.'

★ ★ ★

By the end of the day, Margaret was exhausted.

'I'll make you some coffee,' Louise, Jack's secretary, offered, then grimaced ruefully. 'There's not a lot else for me to do.'

'Thanks.' Margaret mustered a smile. 'I need it. And thanks for staying on. I'm sorry about all this, Louise. You've been great. I don't know how I'd have coped without you.'

'All I've done is send the staff we don't need home and answer the telephone.' Louise shrugged. 'So, what happens now?'

'They've put a hold on all exports and imports,' Margaret told her. 'But once they've checked us out, we should be able to get back to running normally.'

'I don't understand it.' Louise sighed. 'The police were asking the staff all sorts of questions. We don't even export to any of the countries they were talking about — do we?'

'Not directly, no.' Margaret bit her lip. 'They seem to think Jack was using a middleman, a fictitious company . . . to receive our exports and pass them on.'

'But you don't believe that any more than I do,' Louise protested.

'Innocent men don't run,' Denis Brown commented in response as he strolled in and looked around.

'Who says he's run anywhere?' Again

Margaret found herself leaping to Jack's defence.

'Well, he's not here, is he?' Denis held his hands palms upwards. 'Seems to me he's left us to carry the can for his shady deals. So what's going to happen?' He addressed this question directly to Margaret. 'In his absence, I suppose you're in charge. What are you going to do?'

He was making it perfectly obvious that whatever her plans were, she couldn't rely on his help. But she had been prepared for that.

'I'm going to carry on as best I can until I get the go-ahead from the DTI. Then it'll be business as usual. When Jack comes back — ' she emphasised the 'when' ' — I want him to have a business to come back to.'

'You're very loyal.' Denis curled his lip in derision.

'That's why Jack chose her to be his personal assistant — and not you,' Louise remarked dryly.

'He only came in to gloat!' Louise

said crossly when Denis had gone. 'He was probably hoping to find you'd fallen apart. He'd have loved that.'

* * *

Barbara Stanton was physically frail, but her small, bird-like frame hid a will of steel. She had been the driving force behind John Stanton, Jack's late father, and Margaret was sure that Jack had inherited his own determination from her.

In all the time she had known her, Margaret had never seen her so pale and drawn as now.

'Thank you for coming, my dear,' she said as soon as she opened the door. 'Please, come through.'

She led the way along a wide corridor to the sitting room at the back of the house.

It was a pleasant room with the afternoon sun streaming in through the French windows. Beside Mrs Stanton's chair was a thick paperback novel. The older woman noticed Margaret looking at it.

'I've been trying to read.' She managed a small smile. 'But I'm finding it difficult to concentrate.'

'I'm afraid I won't be much help,' Margaret began apologetically. 'It's all such a muddle at the moment.'

They sat down in identical chairs on either side of the French windows. Mrs Stanton smiled briefly, then her expression became sombre again.

'It's so unlike Jack to go off without a word. I'm afraid something awful must have happened. I know that he trusted you. Surely you have some idea . . . ?'

'I'm sorry — ' Margaret began, but Barbara Stanton cut in.

'I understand. Just tell me, Margaret — is he all right?'

'Yes.' She was relieved that Mrs Stanton's question had been so straightforward. There was no need to tell her she'd seen Jack the night before. 'As far as I know.'

Mrs Stanton seemed to crumple as if she'd been fighting her feelings all day.

'I was so afraid,' she admitted softly. 'The police were here asking me all sorts of questions . . . '

Margaret was instantly annoyed. 'They shouldn't have frightened you like that!'

'Oh, I'm sure they didn't mean to,' Mrs Stanton protested. 'They were very polite. The young policewoman even made us a pot of tea!'

'Well, you must try not to worry. And I'll try to keep the business going as best I can until things are sorted out.'

'Oh, thank you, Margaret. I'm sure Jack — wherever he is — will be grateful.'

'And if you want anything, you know where I am,' Margaret prompted gently.

Mrs Stanton rested her hands in her lap, and Margaret noticed they were shaking. She leaned over and gently took the other woman's hand.

'Jack will be all right,' she said firmly. 'The more I think about it, the more sure I am there's a very good reason for what he's doing . . . '

'But he's all alone . . . ' Mrs Stanton said tremulously, and began to cry.

'No!' Margaret was shocked by the proud woman's tears. 'He isn't! He has you — and me — and a lot of other people!'

'I'm sorry.' Mrs Stanton reached into her pocket for a handkerchief. 'I feel such a fool. But he's all I have left. If anything happened to him . . . '

'It won't.' Margaret's voice was firm as she got to her feet. 'I'll go and make some tea. It'll make us both feel better.'

As she filled the kettle, she had a sudden picture of Jack's face, smiling at her the way he did when he was pleased with something she'd done. He had always encouraged her to believe in herself and her abilities . . . I mustn't doubt him now, she told herself firmly.

'There are some biscuits in the tin, Margaret,' Mrs Stanton called from the sitting room.

Margaret poured boiling water into the teapot, then put it on the tray with a plate of biscuits and carried it through.

Mrs Stanton had composed herself.

She looked cool and calm again. Only the redness about her eyes betrayed her true feelings.

'I feel so much better for having talked to you,' she said.

'I just wish I could have been more help,' Margaret protested.

'Just knowing Jack's all right is enough.' Mrs Stanton was smiling now. 'That's all that matters. Now, tell me the latest news about your family. Is your mother still on all those committees?'

* * *

It was dark by the time Margaret left Mrs Stanton's house. She waited until she heard the old lady slide the bolts to secure the front door, then hurried over to her car.

As she left the drive, she noticed headlights switch on farther down the street and a car pulled out behind her.

She kept an eye on the other car in her rear-view mirror. It seemed to be keeping pace with her.

'Are you following me?' she murmured, drawing comfort from the sound of her voice.

If I pull in at the petrol station, she thought, the car will just drive past. And if it doesn't? Well, at least I'll know for sure!

She began to feel angry. The police had been watching Jack. Now they were following her! Maybe they hoped she would lead them to him.

She drove on to the brightly-lit petrol station forecourt. The other car passed — but stopped in the road just outside the petrol station.

Her hand was shaking as she fumbled with her petrol cap, and, while she filled the tank, she kept an eye on the dark car.

It was too far away to identify it . . . but it didn't look like a police car. It looked far too — conspicuous!

She went to the office, paid for her petrol, and left the garage as quickly as she could. When she dared to look, the headlights were still there in her rear-view mirror.

As she drove into the carpark beside her flat, she had already made up her mind to drive straight out again if the car followed. Then she would head for the nearest police station . . .

When she saw it driving past, she almost sobbed with relief.

One of the carpark lights was out, causing ominous shadows. Carefully she avoided them, trying to keep to the lit path. As she hurried along, her heels clacking on the ground, she thought she heard footsteps following behind . . .

Forcing herself to remain calm, she reached the flat door and fumbled for her key, her shaking hands making the simple task difficult.

'Margaret . . . '

A hand fell on her shoulder and she twisted away, heart thudding, ready to run.

'It's all right! It's only me!'

'Bill?' Her whole body went weak with relief.

'Who else would it be?' He took her keys from her and unlocked the door.

'What were you doing? Following me like that?' she demanded crossly.

'Following you? What are you talking about? I've been waiting out here, sitting on the wall.'

She began to tremble and he wrapped his arms around her and held her close, murmuring comforting words as he stroked her hair.

'It's all right now, I'm here . . . '

'I was being followed,' she babbled. 'There was a car . . . '

He looked sceptical. 'Are you sure? The road's pretty busy — don't you think maybe somebody just happened to be driving behind you?'

'No, they were definitely following me. They stopped and waited when I went for petrol.'

'Come on. Let's get inside. You need a drink.'

She looked warily up the stairs and Bill followed her gaze, understanding at once.

'Don't worry. I'll check the flat.'

He went ahead, unlocked her door and walked in, switching on the lights. Margaret followed tentatively.

While he was checking her bedroom, she noticed the light blinking on her answering machine. She pressed the button to replay the messages, and heard her mother's voice.

'Margaret? Darling, what's happening? We're so worried about you. Call me.'

Bill came out of the bedroom and smiled at her.

'No-one here,' he said. 'You'd better call your mother. I'll make some coffee.'

Margaret dialled her mother's number, and the phone was answered almost immediately.

'Darling, we've been so worried,' Jenny Harris said. 'Are you all right?'

It was all Margaret could do not to burst into tears at the comforting sound of her mother's voice.

'I'm fine,' she managed to say at last.

'Here's your father. He wants to

speak to you.' The telephone was passed over.

'Dad? Hello.'

'Hello, love.' Andrew Harris's voice was warm, reassuring. 'Dreadful business. Won't you come home?'

'I can't. I'm going to be very busy . . . while Jack's away.'

'What's the man thinking of — ' her father demanded ' — running off and leaving you to cope with his mess?'

'It's not that simple . . . ' she began, but there was a scuffling noise from the phone.

'Hang on,' her father called. 'Your sister wants a word!'

'Are you out on bail?' her younger sister, Angie, asked.

She'd just finished a course in nursery nursing at the local college and was working at a small nursery school in the village. Working with very young children, she seemed to have retained a kind of childish innocence.

'Don't be daft!' Ben, her brother, sounded impatient in the background.

'Margaret hasn't done anything wrong.'

'The police were very nice to me,' Margaret told her. 'They're just doing their job, after all.'

'Were you scared?' Angie wanted to know.

'Where's Jack disappeared to?' Ben asked.

'What are you going to do?' This was Angie again, and Margaret found herself smiling as she imagined her brother and sister wrestling with the phone to each get their turn.

'I suppose a job at Stanton's is out of the question now then?' Ben complained. He wasn't known for his tact.

Angie was shocked. 'Ben!' she protested.

'Stop it, you two!' Jenny Harris recaptured the phone from them and came back on the line. 'Is Bill with you, Margaret? He called earlier looking for you.'

'Yes, he's here.'

'I'm glad.' She sounded relieved. 'I don't like you being on your own. Are you sure you're all right, darling?'

It was suddenly too much. Margaret couldn't speak, afraid she would burst into tears.

Helplessly she looked up at Bill standing beside her. Gently he took the phone from her hand.

'I'm here, Mrs Harris. We're going to have a drink and then I'm going to take Margaret out for dinner and try to take her mind off things.'

*   *   *

Half an hour later as they were on her way out of the flat, Margaret stopped at the door and glanced back. Jack's packet was still hidden in the cushion.

She'd been worrying about it all day. She wasn't going to let it out of her sight again!

'Margaret . . . ?' Bill's voice drifted back down the hall. 'Are you coming?'

Quickly she removed the envelope and shoved it into her bag, then closed the zip.

'I'm just coming. I — I forgot something,' she explained, blushing guiltily as Bill came back into the living room. She didn't like keeping things from him, but he mustn't know.

They walked the short distance to their favourite Italian restaurant. Margaret didn't feel hungry, but she dutifully studied the menu and chose lasagne.

Then she sat fiddling with the stem of her wine glass, staring into space, lost in a world of her own.

Bill sat watching her for a few moments, then, 'Margaret — ' he began and she turned to him with a faint smile. 'I know I said I wouldn't mention Jack Stanton — but I wondered if all this has made you think again. About my offer, I mean. I wish you'd reconsider coming to work with me.'

Margaret noticed the change. Now he wanted her to work *with* him instead of *for* him. She appreciated that he was trying very hard, but she loved her job . . .

She shook her head and Bill shrugged, accepting her decision.

'I haven't had a chance to tell you.' He broke the silence after a few minutes. 'I heard this morning that I've qualified for a grant from the parish council. It's not much, but it'll help towards the brochures and so on.'

Now that he'd got on to the subject of his folk museum, there was no stopping him, and Margaret let him talk all through the meal, grateful to be thinking about something completely different. She was almost able to pretend that today had never happened . . .

'You haven't eaten much,' he commented finally. 'No appetite? I'm not surprised. You've had a rotten day.'

'It's not all been bad.' She smiled. 'I've enjoyed this evening.'

'Have you?' He looked pleased. 'Still, maybe I should take you home now. You look all in.'

She grimaced. 'I feel it. I hardly slept last night.'

He frowned. 'Last night? But surely none of this came to light until this morning?' His eyes narrowed. 'Are you sure you don't know more than you're letting on?'

Again she felt tempted to confide in him. But what good would it do? He would probably insist she took the envelope straight to the police!

She closed her eyes and felt his hand cover hers.

'Come on — let's get you home,' he said softly.

The evening had turned cooler and she shivered as they left the restaurant. Bill took her arm and tucked it through his. She immediately felt better.

Outside the block of flats, in the shadows of the porch, Bill drew her into his arms. She melted against him, enjoying his gentle goodnight kiss.

'I'll come up,' he murmured as they parted. 'Just to see you safely in. Then I'll be off.'

He held out his hand for her keys, but when he went to open the main door, it swung open at his touch. He turned and glanced at her, frowning.

'That should be locked!' she whispered.

Her heart began to hammer. Thank goodness Bill was here, she thought as they climbed the stairs.

On the landing, she saw the door to her flat was ajar.

Bill put out his hand, motioning her to keep back.

Cautiously, he pushed the door open, reached in and flicked the light switch . . . Then he swore under his breath.

'I think they've gone!' he called seconds later, and Margaret followed him in.

Her belongings were lying all over the floor. Drawers had been pulled out and the contents tipped out, paintings had been torn from the walls and the sofa slashed open . . .

Her clothes were everywhere, tangled on the floor with pots from the kitchen and ornaments from the shelves. Her jewellery box had been emptied and tossed aside . . .

News From Jack!

Later, Margaret stood in the middle of her wrecked living room while Bill saw the police out. She still couldn't believe it had happened.

'How are you feeling?' Bill asked as he came back in.

'Awful,' she admitted. 'Why did they have to make such a mess?'

She gazed around, picked up a cushion from the floor and looked for somewhere to put it . . .

'You can't stay here tonight!' Bill was struggling to control his fury. If he ever got his hands on . . . 'I'll take you home.'

'But I have to tidy up!' Margaret protested weakly. 'I can't leave it like this . . . but where do I start?' There was a note of despair in her voice.

'It can wait,' Bill told her firmly. 'Why don't you go and pack what you need? I'll phone your mum and then make a start on moving some of the heavier stuff.'

'Oh, Bill . . . '

'Don't argue.' He sounded stern, but she could see the tenderness and concern in his eyes.

While she packed, she could hear him righting the furniture and sliding it back into place.

As she picked up a sweater, she shuddered. Thank goodness for Bill. What would she have done without him?

'Ready?' Bill was standing watching her from the bedroom door. 'We ought to be going. It's well past midnight. Your mother will be waiting.'

Margaret took a last look round before closing the door on the flat and locking it. At least the police had been able to arrange a locksmith.

Sitting beside her in the car, Bill tried again to reassure her.

'Try not to be too upset. They didn't take anything of any value, did they?'

She shook her head, and Bill continued to talk, but she hardly heard a word. As the car rushed through the night, she was going over and over what had happened.

She had been surprised when Inspector Travers had turned up at the flat. He obviously suspected the burglary was connected with Jack's disappearance.

'You say nothing's been taken?' he'd said. 'It looks as if they were searching for something. Have you any idea what that could be?'

He must have seen her look of alarm as she clutched her bag — and misinterpreted it.

'It's just a theory at this stage,' he'd said reassuringly. 'You probably disturbed them before they had the chance to take anything.'

* * *

When Bill pulled up outside the familiar house, Margaret sighed with relief. Her parents had left the porch light burning, and it cast a welcoming glow over the front path.

Even before Bill switched off the engine, the front door was flung open and Jenny Harris rushed out, holding her dressing-gown tightly around her. As Margaret stepped out of the car, she wrapped her arms around her.

'Oh, darling . . . are you all right?'

'You shouldn't have waited up, Mum,' Margaret protested, although she didn't try to move. 'It's so late.'

'Did you really think I could sleep until you got here?' Jenny held her at arms' length and had a good long look at her. 'Everyone wanted to stay up — but I put my foot down and sent them all to bed!'

Bill winked at Margaret as he carried her case into the hall.

'Thanks for bringing her home, Bill,' Jenny said. 'Would you like a coffee or something?'

'I'd better not, thanks all the same. I've got work in the morning. I'll pop in and see you tomorrow.' He gave

Margaret a quick hug and kiss, and then he left the two women together.

'Thank goodness he was with you,' Jenny said as the door closed behind him.

Before Margaret could reply, her father came hurrying down the stairs.

'I couldn't sleep! Are you all right?'

Behind him, Ben and Angie appeared and Margaret was suddenly overwhelmed with the sheer relief at being with her family. Just knowing they were there and that they all cared so much made her feel better.

She hugged them each in turn. She couldn't remember ever being so grateful in her life.

'I'll take your bag up to your room,' Ben said gruffly.

'I'll make you some cocoa,' Angie offered. 'Just the way you like it.'

'Did . . . ' her father began, but Jenny shushed him before he could utter another word.

'No questions tonight, Andrew,' she said firmly. 'Margaret looks absolutely shattered. It's straight to bed for her — and straight to sleep.'

'All right,' he agreed, though Margaret could see he was itching to ask questions. 'We can talk tomorrow.'

She kissed them all goodnight and went straight upstairs. She was in bed when Angie came in with her cocoa.

'Dad put a drop of brandy in it. He thought you could do with it.'

'Thanks.' Margaret was feeling wonderfully pampered already.

Angie turned towards the door.

'Mum says I'm not to stay and bother you!' she said with a rueful grin, but at the door she looked back at her sister sitting in the bed, looking so vulnerable somehow, and rushed back to give her a hug.

'Oh, Mags, it must be horrible! First Jack Stanton running off, now this. If there's anything I can do . . . '

Margaret felt tears sting her eyes.

'Thanks, Ange,' she whispered.

Long after everyone else had gone to bed and the house was silent, Margaret sat up in bed staring at her handbag.

'This has gone on long enough!' she decided suddenly. 'I don't care what you said, Jack . . . I'm involved now!'

She got up, opened her bag and took out the envelope. She tore open the flap — and was vaguely disappointed to find it contained just one computer disk.

Surely this one small object couldn't be the cause of so much trouble?

There was no label on the disk . . . she had no idea what information it contained.

But she was determined to find out.

Not tonight, though . . . she crept back to bed and snuggled down under the covers.

★　★　★

She woke up from a fitful sleep just as her mother came into her room carrying a tray. She sat up quickly, forgetting for a moment why she was there. Then the memories of the night came flooding back.

'How did you sleep?' Jenny set the tray carefully on her lap.

'Like a log,' Margaret lied. She'd hardly slept at all for wondering what was on that floppy disk.

She sipped her tea and spread marmalade on her toast. Despite everything, she was ravenous.

'Ben's got a job interview today,' Jenny told her. 'He doesn't hold out much hope — but I said that just getting to the interview stage is an achievement these days.'

'He's bound to feel fed up, Mum,' Margaret replied. 'I mean, you spent all those years telling him how important it was to get a good education and now he has . . . well, he doesn't seem to be much better off, does he?'

'Don't you start talking like that,' Jenny scolded. 'I hear enough of that from him. I'm sure he'll get a job soon. I know he will!'

Jenny was about to go back downstairs, when Margaret remembered the computer disk in her bag.

'Has Dad left for the bank yet?'

'No . . . why?'

'I want a word with him . . . '

Margaret set the breakfast tray aside, jumped out of bed and pulled on her dressing-gown, then grabbed her handbag off the chair.

'Well!' Jenny laughed. 'It must be important! He's in his study.'

Her father's study was a small room off the living room. It was his own private domain, where he could retreat when he needed some peace and quiet.

She knocked and went in. Andrew was packing his briefcase.

'Hello, love.' He looked up, smiling. 'You look better this morning.'

She closed the door behind her.

'Dad — ?' She tried and failed to keep the urgency out of her voice. 'Can I use your computer?'

He looked surprised, but said, 'Of course!'

She put her bag on the desk, drew the disk from the envelope and held it up for his inspection.

'Is this compatible?'

'Let's try it and see. What's on it?' he asked as he switched the computer on.

'I'm hoping you'll be able to tell me,' she returned.

He inserted the disk into the drive and peered at the screen.

'Hmm . . . ' He tapped a few keys, but, 'It's no use. I can't get in. We need a password.'

'Let me try,' Margaret urged.

But the result was exactly the same. She sat looking at the screen. No password — no information.

'I've seen this sort of thing before, love. I expect you have, too. But did you know that if the password has used just ten letters from the alphabet, it would take approximately four hundred years to get into it?'

'Thanks, Dad — that's really cheered me up!'

He stroked his chin thoughtfully.

'We could always try guesswork — '

He tapped in Margaret's name. The computer flashed back *Incorrect Password.*

He took the disk out of the computer and handed it back to Margaret.

'Sorry, love, this could take all morning and I have to go. You could keep trying, though.'

Margaret thought about it. She would have to go to work, too. Could she risk leaving the disk here?

'Dad . . . could I ask another favour? Would you take it to the bank with you and lock it away safely?'

His eyes narrowed suspiciously. 'This has something to do with Jack Stanton's disappearance, doesn't it?'

She grasped his hand.

'Please — don't ask me any questions. You've just got to trust me, Dad.' Hadn't Jack said those very words to her?

'I do, Margaret, but . . . ' He sighed. 'Well, do you really know what's going on? Couldn't you be getting yourself into all sorts of trouble?'

She didn't answer that.

'I just know that Jack's innocent,' she said instead. 'And somehow that disk will prove it!'

'What if it proves his guilt?' Andrew Harris asked softly. 'Have you considered that?'

She hadn't. But she let him take the envelope anyway.

'I take it you've considered handing this to the police?'

She shrugged. 'It wouldn't be any use without the password.'

'OK. I'll lock it up,' he promised.

He was fastening his briefcase when Jenny Harris walked in. She looked suspiciously from her husband to her daughter.

'What are you two up to?'

'Just having a chat.' Andrew chuckled. 'I was trying to persuade her to come back home permanently.'

'Of course,' Jenny agreed at once. 'This will always be your home, Margaret. You're always welcome to come back.'

'I know and I'm grateful,' Margaret said, aware of a huge sense of relief that the disk was out of her hands — but safe.

She kissed her father goodbye, then went with her mother into the kitchen.

Ben was sitting at the table scouring the Situations Vacant column in the local paper.

'You look very smart!' she commented.

'D'you think the tie is all right with this shirt?' he asked anxiously. 'I want to make a good impression.'

Jenny sighed with exasperation. 'I've already told him I don't know how many times that he looks fine!'

Angie was at the sink, washing up and humming along with the radio. Jenny poured out two more cups of tea.

It all felt so normal, so real and warm . . . Margaret felt herself relax at last.

'Anything in the paper?' she asked.

'All the jobs are for care assistants or salesmen.' He looked despondent. 'And they all want experience!'

'What are you going for today?'

He pulled a face. 'Check-out operator at the new supermarket. Wonderful!'

'Well, it would be something at least,

wouldn't it?' Margaret tried to sound enthusiastic. 'Have you ever thought of talking to Bill about a job? He's bound to need staff for the museum.'

'They say you stand a better chance of getting a job if you already have one!' Jenny put in.

'That doesn't make any sense,' Margaret protested. 'At Stanton's, we don't discriminate against the unemployed. Jack's always believed in giving people a chance.'

At the mention of Jack's name, there was a slightly uncomfortable silence. Angie broke it by wiping her hands and saying it was time she got off to work at the day nursery.

'I'll have to go in to Stanford today,' Margaret said when her sister had gone. 'There are a few things I have to attend to at work and . . . and I should do something about the mess in my flat.'

'Then I'll come with you,' Jenny told her firmly. 'I'm not letting you go back there all on your own!'

Margaret knew there was no point in

arguing. Besides, she suspected she would be very glad of her mother's company . . .

* * *

When Jenny walked into the flat behind Margaret and saw the mess, she felt tears sting her eyes. It was far worse than she had expected.

She glanced at Margaret. She had always been so proud of her home, and now . . .

Resolutely she put on a brave face.

'Come on. Let's get going. We'll soon have this sorted. Do you want to start in the living room?'

Margaret bent down and picked up the pieces of a broken china collie. She stared at it for a moment.

'Angie gave this to me as a flat-warming present. Why did they have to break it, Mum?' she added sadly.

Jenny put her arm round her shoulders.

'Why don't you go to work, love? I'll sort out this mess and when you come home it'll all be as right as rain.'

'No! I couldn't let you do that. I — I'll be all right.'

Margaret dropped the pieces into a bin bag and forced a smile as she began to sweep shattered china into a dustpan.

Watching, Jenny felt a surge of anger. But it wasn't at the people who had done this. It was at Jack Stanton! The man who had lured her daughter away from home in the first place with his high-powered job and promises of a directorship!

'Mum — are you all right?' Margaret glanced at Jenny, puzzled by the look in her eyes.

Jenny sighed. 'I can't help thinking you'd be happier if you married Bill and came home! What's so wonderful about working for Jack Stanton anyway? He never did come up with that partnership he talked about, did he?'

'It's been a difficult time ... '

Margaret protested.

'When I met Jack Stanton, he struck me as being a very charming and clever man,' Jenny went on. 'I liked him, but — ' She stared at her daughter thoughtfully. 'But Bill says he doesn't trust him.'

'He's wrong!' Margaret cried. 'Jack's a good man! He's honest and hard working . . . and . . . '

She broke off. It was impossible to explain.

Turning away, she got on with clearing up . . .

★ ★ ★

'It doesn't look the same,' Margaret said when they'd finally finished. The flat looked presentable and clean, but . . . 'It doesn't feel the same.'

'It'll take a while before it's 'yours' again,' Jenny assured her. 'Why don't you just come and stay with us? I don't like to think of you living here on your own after all that's happened.'

'I'm not going to be frightened out of my own home,' Margaret said. 'But — maybe I will stay with you and Dad, just for a little while — so long as you really don't mind.'

'Mind?' Jenny cried. 'Of course we don't mind!'

They left the flat and Margaret drove to the office. There were no police outside this time, just a small group of reporters, who swarmed around Margaret's car as she pulled up at the gates.

Jenny was surprised at the attention and Margaret was relieved when they finally got into the building.

'Mum, I want you to meet Louise Carter — Jack's secretary.' Margaret smiled as the striking young woman emerged from an office. 'Louise — this is my mother.'

'Pleased to meet you,' Louise greeted her warmly. 'Have you been helping Margaret at the flat? I heard about that. It's awful!'

'Yes, it is. And they left it in such a mess! I couldn't let her deal with it on her own. She puts on a brave face, but I know she's terribly upset.'

'It's only natural,' Louise replied. 'She can cope with most things but something like that — well, it's personal, isn't it? Look, I'd better make some coffee. There are some phone messages on your desk, Margaret.'

They moved in to Margaret's office and Jenny looked around, impressed.

'So this is your office! It's better than your dad's at the bank!' she commented.

Margaret shrugged, too distracted to feel proud. 'I told you — Jack takes good care of me.'

'And you've all that work to do?' Jenny looked at the pile of papers on Margaret's desk. 'You'll be at it for hours.' She turned to the door. 'I'll go and do a bit of shopping. And I shan't bother coming back here.' Jenny glanced out of the window. 'Give me your key and I'll meet you back at your flat.'

Margaret and Louise watched as

Jenny strode out of the gate and saw her stop and have words with the reporters.

Margaret shook her head and laughed. 'I bet she won't say anything they can print!' She sighed. 'Seriously, I don't know what I would have done without her today.'

★   ★   ★

She was engrossed in paperwork when Louise put a call through some time and two cups of coffee later.

'It's Mrs Stanton,' she said. 'It sounds urgent.'

As a result of that call, Margaret pulled up outside Mrs Stanton's house later that afternoon. The front door was opened immediately.

'I'm so glad you came!' Barbara sounded a little breathless. 'I was so sorry to hear about the break-in. It must have been dreadful for you. If there's anything I can do . . . '

'That's very kind, thank you,' Margaret said, touched by the woman's concern.

'Why don't you come through?'

Margaret followed her to the sitting room where a tea-tray was already prepared.

Jack's mother was obviously feeling a good deal better. There was a definite brightness in her eyes as she poured two cups and passed one to Margaret. The reason was soon revealed.

'I've heard from Jack!' she declared.

Margaret was so relieved she nearly dropped her cup.

'Is he all right?'

'He didn't say much. He was worried that the call might be traced.' Mrs Stanton frowned. 'So melodramatic! He wouldn't tell me where he is . . . but at least he's been in touch. That's something, I suppose.'

'I wish he'd call me,' Margaret muttered. 'I'd like a few words!'

There was a short silence.

'He gave me a message for you,' Mrs Stanton confessed. 'That's why I asked you to come. He's going to call you at five o'clock.'

They both turned to look at the clock. There was less than ten minutes to go.

'Did he say anything else?' Margaret asked.

'Only the usual. He reminded me to take my pills and told me not to worry! But I'm his mother — how can I not worry?' She threw up her hands in a gesture of despair, then got to her feet 'Come along, my dear. Quickly, now.'

Bemused, Margaret rose and followed her out through the kitchen and into the back garden.

'But the phone . . . ' she protested as she was ushered through a gap in the fence and into next-door's garden.

Mrs Stanton's elderly neighbour was standing at the kitchen door.

'Hurry!' she called when she saw them. 'It's ringing!'

Mrs Stanton grinned impishly.

'I told you — Jack's worried about phone tapping. He said he'd ring Edith's number. Don't worry. You can trust Edie — we've been best friends since primary school! She's Jack's godmother.'

Margaret laughed. 'Do you know, I think you're enjoying all this, Mrs Stanton.'

The phone was still ringing, demanding attention.

'You'd better answer it. It's you he wants to speak to,' Mrs Stanton urged.

Margaret hurried into the hall and picked up the receiver.

Jack's voice came down the line, urgent.

'Mother? Is Margaret . . . ?'

'This is Margaret!' she interrupted. 'Jack, do you realise what's happening here? They've practically emptied the office and I've had to tell most of the staff not to come in to work. I've been questioned by the police and . . . '

'Margaret . . . Margaret,' he interrupted. 'I can guess what's happening, but can you keep things going?'

After everything she'd been through, all he was worried about was whether she could keep the business going! The nerve!

Anger boiled up in her as relief turned to outrage.

'That's what I'm trying to do!' she snapped. 'Have you any idea of the trouble you're in? And your poor mother . . . she's beside herself with worry. How could you do that to her?'

She glanced at Barbara and Edith, who were whispering together like a pair of conspirators, looking anything but worried at this particular moment, it had to be said.

'I wouldn't hurt my mother for the world,' Jack was saying. 'Or you, come to that. But she's a lot stronger than you think and now she knows I'm all right . . . '

'She doesn't know anything of the sort!' she snapped. 'Where are you?'

He didn't reply, and she continued to bombard him with questions he wouldn't answer until, at last, she ran out of breath.

'Finished?' he asked patiently.

'No! There's a lot more I'd like to say to you, Jack Stanton, but it can wait until we're face to face!' she finished.

'Please, Margaret, don't be angry. I know it looks bad, but once I can sort this out . . .'

'Sort what out, precisely? You've either been exporting illegally or you haven't! Which is it?'

'Of course I haven't!' He paused. 'Not knowingly, anyway. I found out that a lot of money has been going through our books — money I didn't know about. I started to investigate our foreign partners and . . . oh, I haven't time to explain right now! Look — please, listen carefully. That envelope I left with you . . .'

'What about it?'

'Is it safe? I should have told you it contains files . . .'

'I know — a floppy disk. I've had a look at it. The information has been encrypted.'

She thought he would be annoyed that she had pried that much, but if he was, he didn't say so.

'I know, I've tried reading it myself.

But so long as it's safe. If it fell into the wrong hands . . . '

'It nearly did,' she admitted, and told him about the break-in.

He listened in silence until she'd finished.

'Margaret, I'm really sorry,' he said quietly. 'It's all my fault. I'm sorry you had to get involved.' For the first time his voice was full of despair. 'You've got to be careful . . . very careful. Don't stay at the flat on your own.'

'I won't . . . ' Especially now she was sure the intruders had been looking for that disk.

'Promise me you'll be careful,' Jack went on. 'Don't take risks. I shouldn't have given that wretched disk to you — but you're the only person I can trust. If you ever think you might be in danger, call the police and tell them everything.'

She tightened her grip on the phone.

'Why can't I just give the disk to the police now?'

'You said yourself, it's useless without the password. Just promise to be careful.'

'I promise,' she whispered at last. 'Jack, when will you be back?'

'I can't come back until I have that password. It's all the proof I need to clear my name. You've just got to trust me.'

'But . . . '

'Please!' A note of desperation had entered his voice and Margaret felt her anger vanish.

'All right. But keep in touch! Your mother's really worried.'

'I'll do my best. If I need to contact you again I'll do it through Edith. But it's difficult to get to a phone. I have to go . . . ' The line suddenly went dead.

'Jack!' Margaret shouted. 'Jack!'

But it was no use. He'd gone.

She put the phone down. Mrs Stanton, alone now, was standing in the doorway, watching her.

'I'm so glad he has you, Margaret,' she said, her eyes filling with tears.

Margaret sighed. It wasn't just Jack who was relying on her now . . .

When she finally got back to her flat,

Margaret found Jenny waiting for her.

'Sorry I was so long!' she apologised.

Jenny was smiling secretively.

'It's all right. I'm only just back myself. I went shopping!'

She pointed to the mantelpiece — where a new china collie had pride of place.

'I know it's not the same, but . . . '

'Oh, Mum!' Margaret hugged her for a moment. 'It's lovely. Thank you . . . '

Her thanks weren't just for the collie. Her mother had just admitted that this was her home now and acknowledged that she would be coming back here to live. Eventually . . .

'Let's go,' Jenny said softly. 'It's been a long day.'

Margaret drove while her mother chatted about her day.

'You know, I'm very proud of you,' she said suddenly, out of the blue.

'Me?' Margaret laughed. 'Well, thank you, Mum.'

'Yes. I hadn't realised how much responsibility you have until today. I suddenly saw you not as my daughter, but as a very competent young businesswoman.'

'That's good to know, Mum.'

Her parents' approval meant a lot.

Margaret was turning the car into the narrow lane leading to the family's isolated house when Jenny exclaimed in annoyance.

'What's that fool doing?' She had just seen a large black car in one of the passing places. 'What a stupid place to park!'

Margaret looked at the car as they passed but the windows were tinted and it was impossible to see inside. Somehow that made it look almost sinister . . .

Once past, she glanced in her rear-view mirror — and saw it pulling out into the lane behind them.

Her grip tightened on the steering wheel. The car was too close. It obviously couldn't get past . . . it was following her!

Jenny, oblivious, chattered on happily.

'Oh, look, Bill's here!' The familiar Land-Rover was parked behind her father's car in the drive.

Margaret parked her own car and Jenny hurried into the house with her parcels.

As she locked the car, Margaret glanced back — and saw the black car again. It was only a few feet away from the end of the drive . . .

She hurried into the house, her heart thundering. Jack had involved her . . . and now she had involved her whole family!

For the first time, she realised how serious the situation was — for all of them . . .

A Glimpse Of Jack

Margaret got into the house just as Jenny was telling Andrew about the car in the lane.

'Stupid place to park!' she told her husband crossly. 'I bet it was a man!'

'Ah, any excuse to get at men drivers!' Andrew chuckled. 'How did your day go? Did you get Margaret's flat straightened out?'

It was all so normal. As Margaret listened to her parents' banter she began to wonder if she was over-reacting, seeing threats that didn't exist.

'Black car, did you say?' Angie asked, looking up from reading a book, peering at them over the top of her rimless reading glasses. 'It's been there for ages. In fact, it gave me a bit of a scare.'

'How do you mean?' Margaret asked sharply.

She glanced at her father and saw he was looking at Angie, concerned.

'What happened?' he prompted.

'When I was walking home from the village, I had to pass it. The electric window whirred down — you know the noise it makes — and I could feel someone staring at me.'

'Did you see anyone?' Andrew's voice was low. 'The driver? Or how many people were in the car?'

'No — and I didn't look back. I was too scared,' Angie admitted.

'Dad,' Margaret said softly, 'the car followed Mum and me right up to the house.'

'What?' her mother cried. 'You didn't tell me!'

'I didn't want to worry you . . . '

Without a word, Andrew and Bill started for the door. Ben, looking bewildered, followed.

'What's going on?' Jenny demanded. 'Who are these people, Margaret?'

'I don't know. I'll go and — ' Margaret headed for the door, but

Jenny put out her hand and held her back.

'No. Let your father and Bill handle it.'

They went to the window and Margaret breathed an audible sigh of relief when she saw the three men coming back up the path to the house. Ben's face was a little pink. He looked relieved — and very young.

'There's no sign of any car now,' Andrew said. 'But I'm going to call Sergeant Richards, just to be on the safe side. I don't like the idea of strangers lurking in the lane.'

'It wasn't the kind of car you'd expect a burglar to use,' Jenny remarked.

'No!' Andrew cast a meaningful look at his oldest daughter. 'That's what worries me.'

Jenny finally made the connection.

'You think it's something to do with Jack Stanton!'

'Of course it is!' Bill sounded angry.

'Let's all calm down,' Andrew said. 'There's probably a perfectly simple explanation. I'll just make that call.'

He was gone from the room for less than five minutes. When he returned, he was smiling.

'Sergeant Richards is going to drive round to take a look. He reckons it was just someone lost. It happens all the time.'

'In a big black limousine?' Bill was scornful.

Jenny took charge. 'I'd better do something about dinner!' she said brightly. 'And we'll have no more talk of big black cars!' she declared.

Margaret and Angie followed her into the kitchen.

'You two can set the table and start the salad. I'll pop the flan in the oven. Then there's soup . . . ' She chattered on to fill the silence.

Margaret watched as Angie set out the cutlery. She seemed unusually clumsy, dropping knives and knocking over the pepper mill. And when a jet from the nearby airbase shrieked overhead, she jumped visibly.

'All they had to do was drive up behind me and grab me and . . . ' she said, shaking. 'No-one would have known what had happened to me!'

'I don't think so,' Margaret tried to reassure her. 'I think they were just trying to frighten you.'

'Well, they certainly succeeded! But I still don't understand why. Why me?'

Margaret turned away. To answer would have frightened Angie even more.

★   ★   ★

'How did you get on at the interview?' Jenny asked Ben brightly as they started dinner.

Ben pulled a face. 'Oh, it was the usual thing. They said they'd keep my name on file, but they reckoned I'm over qualified.'

'More likely they thought you'd scare the customers!' Angie joked, trying to throw off her worries.

'Listen to her!' Ben retorted. 'The

nursery school teacher from the Black Lagoon!'

'Stop it!' Jenny interrupted sharply. 'I won't have you bickering at the table! You're old enough to know better.'

'Sorry, Mum!' Angie said sheepishly.

'How about coming to work for me at the museum?' Bill intervened lightly. 'I'm planning to have working demonstrations — all in period costume. There's a lady going to demonstrate spinning skills and another who can strip and weave willow. With a bit of luck I'm going to get the smithy working . . . And there'll be a wheelwright, too. You'd be surprised how many craftsmen there are around who are only too willing to show off their skill.'

'I'm not a craftsman.' Ben looked downhearted. 'I've no skills worth sharing — or showing. What on earth could I do at the smithy?'

'You've got a way with horses,' his mother pointed out. 'You used to work at the stables at the weekends.'

'Well?' Bill turned to look at Ben. 'What do you say?'

'Well — ' Ben grinned broadly. 'I do love working with horses and . . . and I've always fancied being a smith!'

Margaret was only vaguely aware of the conversation; she was deep in thought, going over Jack's phone call again. Had he said anything that gave a clue to his whereabouts? If only she had some way of contacting him . . .

He'd hung up so abruptly. Was he in danger? She bit her lip and looked up to see her father opening a bottle of wine.

Everyone was laughing and happy. What had happened? What had she missed?

She glanced at Bill and caught him staring at her. He'd seen her faraway look and must have known she was thinking about Jack. She flushed guiltily.

'Wake up!' Angie nudged her. 'Ben's going to work for Bill at the museum!'

'What . . . ? Oh, that's wonderful!' Determinedly she pushed all thoughts of Jack Stanton from her mind and joined in the celebrations.

★   ★   ★

Jack Stanton climbed the stairs of his hotel. He was hot and his shirt clung to his back. All he wanted was to get under the shower and feel cool again.

His mouth felt dry and gritty and the unfamiliar growth of beard itched. If only he could go home . . . He would never complain about the rain again!

When he reached his room, he found the door unlocked and ajar. Cautiously he nudged it wider open with his foot before entering.

Nothing seemed out of place, but someone had been searching through his things. As if he'd be stupid enough to bring the disk with him!

He suddenly felt alone and very frightened. His whole purpose in being here was to prove his innocence. To do that he would have to remain anonymous.

Now someone knew who he was and why he was there. They would never let him get away with it.

Sitting down on the edge of his bed, he tried to think.

He mustn't panic. And he simply mustn't give up. He was almost there . . .

He got to his feet, grabbed his bags and began to pack.

Downstairs in the lobby, he paid his bill and checked out. There was a man sitting by the window, reading a newspaper. He looked up at Jack as he left.

A hot breeze swirled dust into Jack's eyes as he hurried along the narrow streets of stuccoed buildings with red roofs, bleached pink by the relentless sun.

Back home, it would be dinner time. His mother would probably have a tray on her lap in front of the television. And Margaret . . .

How good it had been to hear her voice, even if she was angry with him. If only he could have told her more, but he'd involved her enough already.

He frowned. Her family would take care of her. He'd never met such a close set of people!

He had the feeling that in some ways they disapproved of him. Bill, Margaret's boyfriend, definitely did! He'd always been very protective and, even before all this had started, he'd seemed to think of Jack as some kind of threat . . .

He wished there had been some other way of handling things. But he'd had to make the decision quickly. There had been no time to waste in working out possible consequences . . .

He glanced back over his shoulder and realised the man from the hotel lobby was following him.

He broke into a run, rounded the corner and turned immediately into an alley. The shadows were cool and welcoming.

He kept to the alleys, not knowing where they would lead. The weight of his bags made him breathless. He couldn't keep running for ever.

He dodged behind some large dust-bins and ducked down, holding his breath as his pursuer rushed past. As the footsteps rapidly retreated he came out of hiding, brushed down his trousers, and set off at a casual pace back the way he'd come.

As he emerged at the edge of town, he shielded his eyes from the sun. In the distance, he could see a dust cloud.

He watched for a while until, eventually, a battered old bus appeared, its image shimmering in the heat haze.

He stayed where he was until it drew up beside him and a young man leaned out of the open front window.

'Hey, buddy!' he called. 'Is there anywhere around here we could pick up some supplies?' The accent was American.

'I'll show you if you like,' Jack offered.

'Climb aboard!' the young man invited.

Jack found himself among a dozen or

so young American students.

'You English, buddy?' one asked. 'What's your name?'

He grinned. 'Jack.'

He was reluctant to involve anyone else, but the only way out of the town was on the bus. He couldn't risk going on a train or a service bus, or even hiring a car.

'Would you mind if I hitched a lift?' Jack asked after the students had loaded the bus with fresh supplies.

The driver grinned at him.

'Sure thing, buddy. Welcome aboard!'

★ ★ ★

When all the washing-up had been done, it was time for Bill to leave. Margaret went to the door with him.

'Thanks for giving Ben a chance,' she said as they stood on the doorstep.

'I don't know why I didn't think of it before. He's bright, friendly, good looking. He might end up as one of our most popular attractions!'

Margaret laughed softly. 'Probably!'

'You've been quiet all evening,' Bill said suddenly. 'Is something the matter — apart from the obvious, I mean?'

She longed to tell him about the disk and Jack's phone call, but wasn't sure how he would react. The last thing she wanted was another argument.

She shook her head.

'I suppose it's just the break-in.'

'It's bound to get you down. Did you get the flat cleaned up?'

'Yes. Mum helped.' Margaret smiled. 'She's been great. I . . . I don't know how I'd have coped without her.'

'She's one in a million, your mother,' Bill said. 'My dad always says that when I think of settling down and getting married, I should look at my future mother-in-law to get an idea of what my wife will be like!'

'Oh, Bill . . . '

He laughed. 'I'm sorry! I mentioned the dreaded word again, didn't I?'

Margaret glared at him. He was so sure of himself! So confident that eventually she would agree to marry him. Did he think she was deliberately playing hard to get, making a game of it all?

'Well, slap my wrists and send me to bed without any cocoa!' he mocked.

For a moment Margaret bristled, then she realised he was making fun of himself. The tension was broken and she found herself laughing.

He took advantage of her sudden change in mood and pulled her into his arms and kissed her.

There was no doubting the physical attraction between them. If only it were all as simple as that . . .

She was enjoying his lingering goodnight kiss when she heard a car coming down the lane. She froze. He released her and looked around.

'It's all right.' He sounded as relieved as she felt. 'It's just Sergeant Richards.'

As the police car parked outside, Bill kissed Margaret briefly on the cheek before going to his Land-Rover.

Sergeant Richards grinned. 'Not

rushing off on my account, are you?'

'Early start tomorrow!' Bill turned to Margaret, indicating her car parked behind his. 'Could you let me out?'

'I'll get the car keys. Come in, Sergeant.'

She took him into the house, then came out again to move her car. Bill tooted his horn as he drove off and gave her a cheery wave.

Back inside, Sergeant Richards was sitting in the lounge with her parents, a cup of tea resting on his knee.

'There's no sign of that car,' he was saying. 'I've spoken to one or two other people who'd noticed it, but it appears to have left the area now.'

'So there's nothing to worry about?' Margaret asked hopefully.

Andrew Harris and Sergeant Richards exchanged looks.

'If there's something going on,' Margaret insisted, 'I'd rather know.'

'OK,' the sergeant replied. 'The car stopped at The Swan. The landlord says they came into the bar and asked for

110

directions to this house. They didn't buy a drink — and they appeared to be foreign.'

'From the Middle East?' Margaret whispered.

'What makes you say that?' Sergeant Richard asked, but Margaret just shook her head in reply to his question.

'No. Jeff got the impression they were Latins,' he went on. 'Spanish — maybe South Americans.'

'But that's where Jack . . . ' Margaret began, then stopped herself.

'Go on,' the sergeant urged.

'That's where . . . well . . . our illegal exports were supposed to be headed,' she finished. 'Although, as far as I knew, we had no trade with South America.'

'Fortunately Jeff was suspicious and had the presence of mind to take the number of the car. I've been in touch with Inspector Travers,' Sergeant Richards went on. 'He's sending someone down.'

He finished his tea and stood up,

handing his cup to Jenny.

'Lovely, thank you. Sorry it wasn't such good news,' he added apologetically. 'You've got my number if you're worried. Call me any time.'

★ ★ ★

The next morning, Margaret left early, intending to stop off at her flat on the way to work.

It still felt strange, but a little better than it had the previous day. She picked up the shiny new collie ornament on the mantelpiece and smiled tenderly. Strange how small things could help make everything seem better.

As she was replacing it, the phone rang.

She jumped, then hurried to answer it before her answering machine could cut in.

'Hello.'

Silence.

'Jack, is that you?'

The silence went on and she strained to hear something — anything. There was just a faint crackling sound.

'Who is this?'

She knew she should hang up, but she was frozen, suddenly too frightened to do anything. Then the decision was taken out of her hands — the caller hung up and the dial tone rang in her ear.

She replaced the receiver and backed away. Was someone calling to find out if she was in? She grabbed her bag and rushed out of the flat.

Would she ever feel safe there again?

Then anger took over. How dare anyone make her feel that way about her home!

Fumbling with her car keys as she crossed to the carpark, she dropped them and had to stoop to pick them up — and that's when she caught sight of a pair of black shoes in the midst of the shrubbery. Someone was hiding in the bushes, watching her!

Quickly she unlocked the car, jumped in and sped off. In her rearview mirror, she saw a man dart towards a dark blue car.

'Calm down!' Louise said as she watched Margaret pacing up and down her office. 'Why don't you just call that detective?'

'I'm going to!' Margaret's voice was grim. 'Can you get him for me?'

Within a few seconds, DCI Travers was on the line.

'I'm being followed!' Margaret blurted out at once, her voice betraying her fear. 'I saw him first outside my flat. Then he followed me to the office.'

'Yes.' Ian Travers sounded unsurprised. 'That'll be Watkins.'

'Watkins?'

'DC Watkins. He's keeping an eye on you.'

'You might have told me!' Margaret cried indignantly. 'Have you any idea how frightened I was?'

'I'm sorry, Miss Harris,' he replied. 'I did inform Sergeant Richards that I'd be arranging it. Didn't he tell you? He said he'd see you at your parents' house first thing.'

'He must have called after I left.'

In spite of her anger, Margaret felt extremely relieved.

Inspector Travers was speaking again. 'If you look out of your window, you should see him parked outside. I've got another man with your parents in case they show up there again. By the way, I did a check on that car last night. It had false number plates.'

Margaret took a few seconds to take it all in.

'So you really think I'm in danger.' Her voice was small.

Travers hesitated.

'Let's just say I'm just not prepared to take any risks. I'm sorry you were frightened by Watkins,' he conceded. 'He's really quite harmless — and there for your own good.'

'And to stop me disappearing, too?' she suggested wryly.

'Just doing my job, Miss Harris,' he returned, non-committal.

'What about the investigation?' she asked. 'Are you getting anywhere?'

'I'm not at liberty . . . '

'Oh, come on! I think I'm entitled to know what's happening. Jack's innocent. You should be trying to find out who is responsible instead of . . . '

'That's exactly what I'm doing, Miss Harris.' The chief inspector was unmoved. 'Now, if you'll excuse me . . . '

When she'd hung up, she saw Louise watching her.

'Are you all right?'

Wordlessly Margaret nodded.

'Sure? If you want to go back to your parents' I'll manage here.'

'No. I'm fine, really.'

Margaret went to the window, looked out and saw the dark blue car parked across the street. The driver looked up and waved. Hesitantly, she waved back.

'Well, as you're staying, you'd better see this,' Louise was saying. 'Remember Portmans gave you twenty-four hours to get Jack's signature?'

'Portmans? Goodness, yes — though that seems about a hundred years ago!'

Louise flapped a letter at her.

'This came this morning. They've cancelled.'

'Oh no. Could you get them on the phone for me, please?' Margaret asked briskly. 'I'll see if I can get them to change their minds.'

Ten minutes later, she was hanging up the phone feeling completely disheartened. As far as the other company was concerned, Jack was guilty on all charges.

'No good?' Louise asked as she put a cup of coffee down on the desk.

Margaret shook her head hopelessly.

'Mud sticks. And until Jack does something to clear his name, it's going to go on sticking.'

'There's more, I'm afraid,' Louise told her. 'I've made a list of the clients who say they're taking their business away.'

'Well, I suppose we can't blame them for that. But I don't have to let them go easily, do I?' Margaret added with determination.

She spent the rest of the morning on

the telephone and eventually had managed to win back at least half the clients.

She worked on through her lunch hour, determined to persuade people that Stanton's was still a company to be trusted.

By four o'clock she was exhausted, but at least she had had no small success. But there was still something she wanted to do.

'I'm going to call in and see Mrs Stanton on my way home,' she told Louise. 'I'll see you tomorrow.'

★ ★ ★

To Margaret's surprise, it was Edith, Barbara's next-door neighbour, who answered the door when she rang the bell.

'I had to call the doctor this morning,' she explained, shaking her head 'It's all this worry.'

'Is Mrs Stanton all right?'

'Oh, she will be. It's her angina — it

was the worst I've ever seen her. She was annoyed with me for calling the doctor but . . . '

'Is that Margaret?' Barbara Stanton's voice drifted downstairs. She certainly sounded all right.

'Yes,' Edith called back. 'I'll send her up.'

When Margaret went upstairs, she found Mrs Stanton sitting up in bed, looking furious.

'Silly woman,' she muttered. 'I told her just to get my pills but she panicked and called the doctor!'

'She was worried about you,' Margaret said, and she knew she sounded reproachful, a tone Mrs Stanton picked up on.

'I know,' the older woman sighed. 'I should be grateful. She's a good friend to me.'

'Have you heard any more from Jack?' Margaret asked.

Barbara Stanton shook her head, looking concerned. 'I was hoping he'd call today.'

'You still don't have any idea where he could be?' Margaret pressed.

'I wish I did! Although the days when I'd go chasing after him are long gone! Of course, there'd be nothing to stop you . . . ' She gave Margaret a long, searching look.

That had never occurred to Margaret. Going to Jack. But at the moment it was academic when she had no idea where he was.

'I *have* to figure out where he's gone. Can you think of anyone he might be staying with?'

'Friends, you mean?' Mrs Stanton said. 'I've already tried everyone I could think of. They nearly all wanted to help — they didn't for a minute believe what they'd been reading in the papers, of course — but they're as much in the dark as I am. I've even spoken to some of his old girlfriends. And one or two current ones!'

Margaret looked up, surprised. Perhaps she hadn't known Jack so well after all. He'd certainly made a point of keeping his business and private lives firmly apart.

'There was never anyone serious,' Mrs Stanton added quickly. 'Not really.' She looked wistful.

'Is there anything I can do while I'm here?' Margaret asked.

'No. Edie's taking care of me.' Mrs Stanton smiled. 'Spoiling me — I don't deserve it!'

'Quite right!' Edith came into the room carrying a tray. 'I thought you'd like a cup of tea, Margaret.'

'Lovely, Edith, thank you.'

When Edith had gone, Mrs Stanton went back to her subject.

'Jack was never one to make friends easily. As a little boy he seemed to spend more time with his dog than with other children. He finds it difficult to let other people get close to him. Even now, he has a very small group of people he'd call real friends — and a lot of acquaintances.'

Margaret sipped her tea, finding it hard to imagine Jack as a small boy.

'Did you ever meet Susannah?' Barbara Stanton was saying.

'Susannah?' Margaret frowned, sifting through her memory. 'No, I don't think so.'

'Beautiful girl.' Mrs Stanton sighed. 'I suppose she was the closest Jack ever came to settling down. I thought she might have called me, but I haven't heard a word from her.'

'Do you think maybe he's with her?' Margaret's mouth had gone dry and she didn't know why.

'Possibly — but I've no idea where.' She sighed. 'I've looked in his room, but I couldn't find anything.'

'His room?'

'Yes. He still comes to stay here now and then even though he has his own place. Why don't you go and have a look? The police already have — but you may spot something they overlooked. It's the room directly opposite this one.'

Margaret got up, crossed the landing, and pushed open the door.

She went to the bed and sat down on the home-made patchwork cover. On the bedside table stood two framed photographs. One was of a dog, the other of a young woman with long blonde hair and sparkling blue eyes. There was writing across the bottom left-hand corner of the picture. *All love, always, Susannah.*

She was very beautiful . . .

Margaret picked up the second picture. The dog was a brindle boxer with a black face.

'He came home in tears once because some children had laughed at Benji — said he was ugly.' Edith's voice said from behind her. 'He was soppy about animals — always bringing home strays.'

When Margaret looked up at Edith, she saw her eyes were glittering with tears.

'I just came up for the tray,' the older woman told her. 'Barbara's dozed off. When you've finished just slip out quietly. I'll tell her you said goodbye.'

'Did you know Susannah?' Margaret asked quickly.

'Oh, yes. A lovely girl. Jack was very fond of her.' Edith smiled and went out, closing the bedroom door behind her.

Margaret put the picture down and picked up a battered old teddy bear.

His original eyes had gone and a pair of black buttons had been sewn on in their place. He was obviously a much-cuddled bear.

Shelves groaned under the weight of dozens of books. More were stacked on the floor, still more on a small desk in the corner. There were stamp albums and photograph albums . . .

She opened one and saw a picture of a teenage boy. He looked so thin and gawky, with a huge smile.

There were more pictures. Girl-friends, holiday snaps, more of Jack as he grew into the man she knew. Or had thought she knew.

Was he really lonely? He always seemed so strong, so outgoing and confident . . . Was it really all an act?

She placed the albums back where she'd found them and, as she did so, a small, battered address book caught her eye. She picked it up, opened it.

Her eyes widened. For someone who was supposed to have few friends, it was crammed full of addresses, the writing ranging from the untidy scrawl of a young boy to the more sophisticated writing of a man.

She put the book in her bag, sure Mrs Stanton wouldn't mind.

As she left the room she was more determined than ever to help Jack.

A Terrible Dilemma

Margaret was reassured by the presence of the dark blue car behind her as she drove home. Poor old Watkins. He must have been bored stiff watching her all day!

She'd made up her mind to ask him in for dinner, but as she pulled into the drive her mother came dashing out of the house.

As soon as the car stopped Jenny pulled open the door.

'Have you seen Angie?' she asked urgently.

Margaret felt her blood chill.

'No. Isn't she home yet?'

'No, though she should have been back ages ago!' Her mother was distraught. 'I keep thinking about that car yesterday.'

'Have you called the police?' Margaret interrupted.

The woman looked stricken, as if she had been hoping Margaret would somehow have a good reason for Angie's lateness.

'Oh, Margaret — should I?'

Margaret didn't answer directly, instead asking, 'Where's Dad?'

'He stays late at the bank on Wednesdays — staff training. And Ben's been with Bill all afternoon at the museum. Oh, where can she be?' Jenny wailed.

'I don't know. But there's a policeman in a car in the lane. I'll go and speak to him.'

'What?' Jenny's voice was a whisper. 'You don't think . . . ' She gripped her daughter's arm.

'I'm sure there's a perfectly simple explanation for her being late,' Margaret lied. She was as frightened as her mother, but forced a smile. 'Try not to worry, Mum.'

'I'm so glad you're home,' Jenny told her fervently. 'Somehow, I don't feel as scared now.'

Margaret squeezed her hand. She'd never imagined having to reassure her mother. And she wished with all her heart it didn't have to be now . . . that it didn't have to be about Angie.

She had a sudden picture in her mind of her sister, sitting at the table reading, her rimless glasses making her look so young, so innocent . . .

If anything happened to her, she would never forgive herself . . . But for her mother's sake, she had to stay calm.

'Don't worry . . . ' She fought to keep her voice level. 'You know Angie. She's probably met someone in the village.'

'But she usually rings if she's going to be late . . . ' Jenny was still anxious, and Margaret was beginning to feel panic.

She forced a reassuring smile. If only Angie would walk through the door . . . If only the phone would ring and she would hear her sister's voice . . .

'I'll tell you what, I'll nip out and see if there's any sign of her coming down the lane.'

She was about to open the front door

when the telephone rang. They looked at each other, then both rushed towards the hall table. Mrs Harris reached it first.

'Hello . . . Angie?'

Margaret watched her mother's face. She was frowning . . .

'Who is this?' she cried suddenly. 'What do you want?'

'Mum . . . ' Margaret took a step nearer.

'He wants to talk to you.' Dully her mother passed over the receiver. 'He won't say who it is.'

Her eyes fixed on the older woman's anxious gaze, Margaret took the phone.

'Hello?' She tried to keep her voice firm and controlled.

'Good evening, Miss Harris,' came a man's voice. 'Just a call to say that your sister is quite safe — and will remain so as long as you co-operate.'

He sounded so sure of himself it was frightening. Glancing at her mother, standing beside her, Margaret tried to keep calm.

'Are you still there, Miss Harris? I hope you are listening to me!' There was a trace of an accent, but not one that she could place.

'Yes, I'm listening.' She was having difficulty breathing. 'How can I help you?' she managed at last.

'I think you know what I want, Miss Harris.'

'What? I'm not . . . ' she stammered.

'Don't!' The voice took on a menacing edge. 'Don't play games with me, Miss Harris.'

'I'm not!'

Jenny reached out to touch Margaret's arm, her face a picture of disbelief.

'The disk,' the man reminded her. 'You know the one I mean?'

'Yes, I do. What about my sister?'

'She's quite safe — for the moment.'

'What do you mean?' Margaret couldn't hide the panic in her voice.

'Exactly what I say. You give us the disk — we give you your sister. It's perfectly simple.'

Margaret bit her lip.

'All right. I'll get it for you.'

'Excellent. You're wise to co-operate.' The caller laughed. 'Now, listen carefully. There's an old stone bridge in the village . . . '

'Yes, I know it,' Margaret put in quickly. 'What time?'

'Eleven o'clock tonight.'

'You don't get anything until I see my sister.' She allowed her rage to spill over for a moment. 'Do you understand?'

'You'll see her — provided you do exactly as I tell you.'

'Let me talk to her!'

'That isn't possible right now. But you have my word she is quite comfortable.'

'Your word?'

'I'm afraid that's going to have to be good enough. And you won't even think about calling the police — will you, Miss Harris?'

He paused, taking her silence for assent.

'Then goodbye, Miss Harris. Until eleven o'clock.'

'Wait!' she cried. 'I want to speak to Angie!'

The line clicked and went dead.

As she turned from replacing the receiver, her mother grasped her arm.

'You've got to tell me what's going on!' she insisted.

'I know, I'm sorry, Mum. But, first — Angie is safe.' She *had* to believe that!

'Where is she? I don't understand! Why wouldn't that man tell me? Why did he insist on speaking to you?'

'I have something they want,' Margaret said slowly.

'That's ridiculous. What can you possibly . . . ?'

'Before he disappeared, Jack left something with me . . . ' she explained.

'Jack?' Jenny went very still. 'Jack Stanton?' Two bright spots of red appeared on her cheeks. 'I should have known!'

'It's a computer disk,' Margaret went on. 'With all the information Jack needs to prove his innocence. But it's encrypted. It has a password . . . '

Miserably her voice tailed off. What could she say? She felt so guilty and ashamed. Angie was in danger — and she was to blame.

'How could you get yourself mixed up in such a mess?' Jenny was furious. 'How could you let it involve your sister?'

'Angie will be all right, Mum,' Margaret promised. 'All we have to do is keep calm and . . . '

'Keep calm! My daughter has been kidnapped and you're telling me to keep calm? We have to call the police right now! Where's that detective?'

She started for the door, but Margaret reached out and held her arm.

'No, Mum. I promised I wouldn't go to the police. If they're watching the house . . . '

'Watching the house?' There was a shocked silence as the colour drained from Jenny's face. 'Will — will they hurt her?'

'It won't come to that,' Margaret said quickly. 'I'll do as they say. By midnight, Angie will be home. I promise.'

Jenny turned and went back into the living room, where she subsided into an armchair.

'We'd better tell your father . . . '

'I'll ring him. I hope he's still at the bank.'

Jenny glanced at the clock on the wall.

'It's late — he may have left,' she replied, then realised there may be more to Margaret's comment than she thought. Her eyes narrowed.

'If he's on his way home he'll hear the news soon enough — so why do you hope he's still at the bank? Is he involved in this somehow now too?'

'Just trust me, Mum, please,' Margaret pleaded, wishing she hadn't asked.

For the first time, she realised how desperate Jack must have been when he asked her to trust him. It wasn't an easy thing to ask someone — especially when you couldn't be sure how things were going to turn out.

She dialled the bank's number and was relieved when her father answered the phone.

'You've just caught me. I was just about to lock up and leave,' he said. 'What's up?'

Margaret took a deep breath, trying to keep her voice light and choosing her words very carefully in case someone else was listening.

'I was just wondering . . . that account you opened for me . . . could you close it and bring me what's in it?'

'Account?' She could imagine his puzzled frown as he tried to work out what she was talking about. 'What account?'

'You remember.' Her voice was shaking now. 'The bonus I got from work.'

For a tense moment there was silence.

'Oh, that account! Of course, no problem. I'll be home soon.'

'Dad . . . ' She couldn't keep it up. She bit her lip to stop the tears. 'Oh,

Dad, please hurry!'

'I'll be there as soon as I can,' he promised, alarmed by her distress.

'Dad — be careful!' she urged — but he had already hung up.

She joined her mother at the window.

'I still think we should tell that policeman,' Mrs Harris said. 'He'll know what to do.'

'No. We have to do exactly as we're told . . .'

She put her arms around her mother and hugged her tight.

They were still standing together when her father's car pulled up outside the house.

Taking a deep breath, Margaret went to meet him at the door. How could she find the words to tell him the dreadful consequences of her actions . . . ?

★　★　★

'What are you doing out of bed?' Edith scolded as Barbara came slowly into her hall. 'You're supposed to be resting!'

'Don't fuss,' Barbara protested crossly. 'Jack's my son. I have to speak to him.'

Edith bustled away to find a chair.

'Well, if you're going to wait for him to call, you'll at least sit down to do it!'

'Thank you.' Barbara sank gratefully on to the chair she brought back. 'What time did he say he'd ring?'

'I wish I'd never told you!' Edith grumbled. 'He just said it would be about tea-time. He didn't want to speak to you — just to know how you were, that's all. He's worried . . . '

'You shouldn't have told him I wasn't well!' Barbara retorted. 'As if he hasn't enough to worry about . . . '

As she spoke, the phone rang. Edith picked it up.

'Hello? Yes — just hold on for a moment, dear . . . '

She smiled and passed the receiver to Barbara who cradled it against her ear.

'Jack . . . ?'

'Mum! Edith says you're ill . . . '

'Just a touch of angina, dear,' she told him calmly, with an accusing look at her friend. 'Nothing to worry about. The doctor has been and I've been resting in bed all day. I feel quite all right now.'

'Are you sure . . . ?' Jack didn't sound convinced.

'Quite sure. You know how Edith fusses,' she added confidingly.

'You must take care of yourself, Mum,' Jack said gently. 'Let Edith help if she wants to.'

'I know. I'm very lucky really . . . ' She grinned in her friend's direction.

'Have you seen Margaret?' Jack asked.

'Of course! She was here earlier today.'

'And she's all right?'

'She's fine.'

'When you see her again, tell her . . . tell her I'm very close to finding the person who can prove I'm innocent.'

Barbara gripped the phone tighter. She had thought, when her son grew up, that she wouldn't have to worry about him any more. How wrong she'd been!

'Where are you, Jack?'

'You'll never believe this.' He laughed softly. 'I'm camping under the stars with a bunch of American students!'

'What? Oh, good — you're not alone! You *are* being careful?'

'You know me! I'm the biggest coward around. I'm not taking any risks.'

'I wish I could believe that. You're very like your father. He seemed to thrive on danger.'

'I'll take that as a compliment!' His voice softened. 'Don't worry. I'll be back soon — all in one piece, too!'

'Can't you tell me where you are?' she persisted. 'I suspect you're abroad somewhere but . . . '

'Don't try playing detective,' Jack interrupted. 'It's better if you don't know.'

'I'm worried sick about you,' she said sternly.

'I know — and I'm sorry. But everything will be all right, I promise.'

'I've always known when you're lying, Jack,' she murmured. 'You're lying now to protect me, aren't you?'

He was silent for a little while.

'I take after you then, don't I? Just a little angina attack — really?'

'Medium,' she conceded. 'Please be careful, Jack . . . '

'I will, I promise.'

★ ★ ★

'So did you bring the disk, Dad?' Margaret finished urgently. Andrew was stunned by what she had told him. He looked at his wife and saw she was pale and anxious, her hands trembling. He reached out and covered them with his own.

He asked the obvious question. 'Have you called the police?'

'No — I didn't dare risk it. I'm sure they would know right away if I did.'

'And you're to meet them at the bridge — when?'

'Eleven tonight.'

'I'll come with you.'

'I have to go alone.'

He looked at her for a long moment, deep in thought, then said, 'They've got Angie. I'm not letting them get you, too!'

'If you're going, then so am I,' her mother put in.

'For goodness' sake,' Margaret snapped. 'This isn't a family outing!'

They all stared at each other.

'I just want to be there — to know you're both safe,' Jenny explained.

'I know, Mum,' Margaret said gently. 'And I do understand — but if I just do as I'm told I'll be all right.'

Andrew opened his case, took out the disk and stood looking at it.

'Whoever would have thought a little thing like this . . . '

'You knew about this all along, didn't you?' Jenny's voice was tight and bitter. 'How could you, Andrew?'

Margaret stared at the disk. Jack had trusted her with it and now she was going to give it away. She closed her eyes and prayed he would understand.

★ ★ ★

It was very hard to appear normal as they sat down to dinner with Ben and Bill and the two young men talked enthusiastically about the museum.

Ben had had a wonderful day and was looking forward to working for Bill. In fact, he'd talked about nothing else since they'd arrived.

'Where's Fishface?' he asked, noticing for the first time that his sister was missing.

'Don't call her that!' Margaret cried angrily.

'They're always calling each other silly names.' Andrew's voice was firm. 'It doesn't mean anything.'

'Why so touchy, Mags?' Ben asked her.

'I . . . I just don't think it's very nice to call people names.' She pushed her plate away. 'I'm sorry — I'm not very hungry, Mum.'

'Are you all right?' Bill's eyes narrowed as he looked at her.

'It's been a long day,' she answered briskly, but she knew he didn't believe her.

She'd known it would be difficult to hide what had happened from Bill, but they'd agreed not to tell him or Ben about Angie. She hated deceiving him . . .

She looked up and saw him still watching her. Thankfully, Ben started talking again.

'We went to an auction. Bill had his eye on a particular horse, but . . . ' He grinned. 'It wasn't the horse you bought in the end, was it?'

'Leave it out, Ben!' Bill was evidently embarrassed.

'You'll never guess what he got instead.' Ben looked around the table gleefully. 'Donkeys! Honestly! He's got four of them.'

'Rescued ex-beach donkeys,' Bill explained. 'Poor things. I know they're nothing to do with the history of the farm, but . . . '

'You've always had a soft spot for donkeys,' Margaret recalled.

'They'll not eat much and they're friendly,' he went on. 'And children will enjoy petting them.'

'You're a kind man, Bill,' she murmured.

Tears weren't far away, but she still couldn't tell him. For all his kindness, he also had a quick temper. And he would certainly never let her go to this meeting alone!

Later, when they said goodnight on the doorstep, Margaret was still preoccupied. Bill realised she wasn't listening to him and heaved a sigh of exasperation.

'Why don't you tell me what's wrong?'

It was hard to resist his gentle, kind voice, but . . .

'I just . . . Oh, I don't know. You're a good man, Bill. You deserve better than me.'

'Probably!' He laughed. 'But I'll make do with what I've got.'

'Ben seems keen to start at the centre,' she commented, getting on to safer ground. 'Thanks for giving him the chance.'

'I think it's going to be fun working

with my future brother-in-law!'

Margaret was so lost in thought, she hardly heard his remark, and her lack of reaction worried him even more.

'Hey.' He caught her chin with his finger and tilted her face up. 'What is it? What's wrong? Surely you can tell me?'

'It's nothing,' she mumbled. 'I'm just tired, that's all.'

His raised eyebrows illustrated his scepticism.

'I don't believe you — and I'm not leaving here until I get an explanation!'

'An explanation!' Margaret spluttered. 'Just who do you think you are?'

'I'm the man who loves you — and I'm worried about you!'

'You've no need — not about me!' she flung at him. 'I just wish you'd stop trying to run my life for me. Keep out of it, Bill!'

'Keep out?' he cried angrily. 'What are you talking about? I'll do no such thing!'

'Look, why don't you just go?' she snapped. 'I'm sick of your possessiveness!'

He stared at her. 'Possessive? Me?'

'Oh, Bill, I don't need this right now. Just . . . go . . . will you?'

'All right! I will!'

As he swung on his heel and marched out to his car, his back rigid, Margaret hugged her arms about herself and wished she could take back her harsh words . . .

Once he'd driven off she returned to the living room and found everyone preparing for an early night. It was a pretence, of course, for Ben's benefit.

'Aren't you going to wait up for Angie?' he asked.

'She's staying the night with Emma,' Andrew answered quickly. 'Off you go, son. You've had a busy day.'

'I was going to watch the film . . . '

'Tape it!' Jenny instructed firmly.

Face To Face

Margaret crouched in the shadows of the hedge beside the garden path, watching anxiously as her mother went out to speak to the young policeman in his car.

Jenny tapped on the window and Ken Watkins woke with a start.

'Mrs Harris?' He sat up abruptly. 'Is something wrong?'

'I was just thinking you don't look very comfortable in there. Wouldn't you like to come inside? You could stretch out on the sofa.'

'That's very kind of you, Mrs Harris, but no, I'd best not. My guv'nor would have a fit if he found out I'd been sleeping on the job!'

'Would he have to know?'

'Oh, he'd know! He knows every-thing,' he commented ruefully.

Margaret tried to see her watch.

Come on, Mum!

'Well, would you like to come in for some hot soup and sandwiches?'

'Oh, I really . . . ' He hesitated. 'It's very late. I don't want to keep you up or anything.'

'You'll be able to keep an eye on things just as well from the kitchen as from out here,' Jenny went on persuasively.

He waggled his head thoughtfully.

'Well, ten minutes wouldn't matter, I suppose. And I *am* starving!'

'There you are then!' Jenny smiled and stepped back as he opened the car door.

Margaret held her breath as he followed her mother into the house and her mother very deliberately closed the door behind him.

Now . . . it had to be now. She ran down the drive and along the lane to where her father had left his car.

When she reached it, her hands were shaking so much she could hardly push the key into the lock. At last, the central locking system opened noisily. Jerking the door open, she slid behind the wheel and started the engine. She waited until she was out of sight of the house before switching on the headlights.

As she drove through the village she saw Bill's Land-Rover parked outside and sighed wistfully. If only she could talk to him . . .

She found herself unconsciously slowing down but then she came to her senses and accelerated again. She had to do this herself.

In daylight, the area around the old stone bridge was a popular beauty spot and picnic place. There was a carpark nearby, hidden by trees.

The car bumped and bounced across the uneven stony ground. As was to be expected at this time of night, there was only one other car in the car park, in a far corner.

Pulling up several yards from it, Margaret switched off the engine with a shaking hand. Taking a deep breath, she tried to compose herself.

Picking up a padded envelope from the passenger seat, she got out of the car at the same time as a man climbed out of the other one.

'Stay where you are, Miss Harris!'

The headlights of the other car came on and Margaret found herself dazzled by the glare of them.

'Where's my sister?' she demanded.

'Have you got the disk?'

'As soon as I see my sister!' she insisted bravely.

'Hold your hands above your head and come forward.'

Margaret did exactly as she was told. Blinded by the headlights, she couldn't see the man's face, but she saw him hold out his hand.

'I'll take the envelope.'

Her heart sank. What else could she do now?

'The disk, Miss Harris!' he prompted.

'Not till I see Angie!' she repeated desperately.

He went to the back of the car and

opened the door and she could see her sister sitting inside, white-faced and minus her glasses.

'Angie ... are you all right?' Margaret's voice was sharp with relief.

The girl looked terrified, but before she could answer, the door was slammed shut again.

'The disk, Miss Harris,' the man insisted.

She handed over the envelope. I'm sorry, Jack, she thought dismally.

'Now let my sister go,' she demanded.

She saw the man's head move, as if he was shaking it.

'Not so fast. How do we know this is the right disk? You might be trying to deceive us, Miss Harris.'

'I'm not. I promise! I didn't even — ' Her voice tailed off.

He handed the disk to someone in the front of the car. As the interior light came on, Margaret could see another man opening up a lap-top computer. He slipped the disk into the drive.

She tried to see Angie to reassure her

that the nightmare would soon be over — but it was impossible.

'I've given you what you want,' Margaret said, after what seemed like an eternity. 'Can we go now? Please!'

'Be patient,' the first man said calmly. 'This won't take long.'

Her mouth felt dry. Surely her father wouldn't have swapped disks?

The man in the car said something in a low voice and the man beside her turned to her.

'That's fine, Miss Harris. Now give me the copy.'

'Copy? What copy?' she cried, her voice rising. 'That's all Jack gave me!'

'Don't take us for fools.' He grabbed her arm and shook her. 'I want the copy!'

'I don't have a copy I tell you!' She was beginning to panic. 'Let me go! I've kept my part of the deal, now you keep yours!'

His grip tightened, his fingers biting into her flesh. She twisted and tried to hit out at him, but he grabbed her wrist.

As they struggled, she heard another vehicle approaching. Two bright white headlights hurtled towards them out of the darkness. A car screeched to a halt beside them.

'Hey! Let her go!' Bill's voice bellowed.

Margaret was thrown aside as the man leapt into the car. It was already moving and she watched in horror as it accelerated across the carpark. Within seconds, its red tail lights disappeared beyond the trees.

Bill turned to Margaret.

'Are you all right? Did they hurt you? Thank God I got here in time . . . I saw you drive past the pub . . . '

Margaret was speechless with pain and shock. Then the reality of what had happened came rushing in.

'You stupid ass!' she cried, pushing him away. 'Now see what you've done!'

Bill's face became puzzled and confused.

'What . . . ?' he began. 'I don't understand.'

'Now they've got Angie *and* the disk!'

He grasped her shoulders, turning her to face him.

'What do you mean? Who's got Angie?'

Margaret flinched and Bill loosened his grip, his tone changing to one of concern.

'Are you hurt? Who were those people? What did they do to you?'

Margaret tried to wriggle free of his grip, but he held her firmly.

'Let me go! It would have been all right if you hadn't interfered!'

Finally Bill released her, his hands dropping to his sides. Even in the darkness, unable to see his face clearly, Margaret knew she'd wounded him.

'I'm sorry . . . I didn't mean — ' she began, but Bill interrupted.

'We'll have to call the police.' His voice was tight.

'No!'

'But they — whoever 'they' are — have got your sister! We've got to do something.'

'I *was* doing something, until you — '

A sound nearby made them both suddenly stop and hold their breaths. A dry twig cracked somewhere in the stillness.

'What . . . ?' Bill began, but Margaret shushed him.

It was she who saw her sister first, just a dark shadow stumbling out of the darkness towards them.

'Angie!' she cried, starting towards her.

Angie was sobbing. Margaret held her tight, unable to stop her own tears from flowing.

For a long time, the two sisters stood where they were, holding each other. Then gently Margaret pushed Angie away, holding her at arm's length, trying to see her in the darkness.

'Where are your glasses?' Tenderly she brushed a strand of hair away from her sister's face. 'Did they hurt you? Are you all right?'

Without waiting for an answer, she hugged her again. Now, both girls were laughing with sheer relief.

'I think we should get as far away from here as possible.' Bill's voice sounded strained.

Margaret shivered. 'You're right.'

She kept her arm tightly around Angie and turned towards the car, but Bill took the keys from her shaking hands.

'You're in no state to drive. It'll be safe enough here until the morning,' he said, locking it. 'Come on, I'll take you home.'

For once Margaret was thankful to let him take over.

* * *

As he helped Angie into his Land-Rover, Bill turned to Margaret and there was no mistaking the determination or the concern in his voice.

'Once I've got you home, I want an explanation.'

She nodded. She owed him that, at least.

The girls sat in the back of the car, holding hands tightly.

'Are you sure they didn't hurt you?' Margaret was almost motherly in her concern for her sister.

'No — but they said something about Jack,' Angie whispered. 'They know where he is and now they have the disk, he's — expendable.'

Margaret gasped in horror. Surely they couldn't mean — ?

'I wish I could warn him,' she muttered fervently.

'How?' Angie asked.

'I don't know,' Margaret admitted. 'Bill . . . don't drive up to the front of the house! I don't want that policeman asking awkward questions!'

Bill let out a sigh of exasperation.

'Just which side of the law are you on?'

But he did as she asked and parked the car in the lane.

They made their way across the back garden to the house and went in through the back door.

Jenny had been sitting at the kitchen table nursing her umpteenth cup of

157

coffee, but she rose to her feet when she saw Margaret, and darted round the table at the sight of Angie to envelop the girl in a tight hug.

'Oh, Angie, love! Thank goodness you're safe!'

Andrew Harris heard the commotion and appeared from the other room, his face tense and white. As Margaret watched, he seemed to go limp and she knew he was experiencing the same sense of relief she had felt.

He put his arms around them both, closing his eyes in silent gratitude.

Margaret glanced at Bill and caught the raw emotion in his eyes. It looked as if he was being torn apart.

It was Jenny who finally broke the embrace.

'Come on — let's get you to bed.'

Keeping her arm round Angie she led the girl from the room, speaking softly to her, asking questions, trying to reassure her that the ordeal was over.

'We've been so worried,' Mr Harris said.

Margaret knew it was a vast under-statement. Suddenly her knees felt weak and she had to sit down quickly.

'I'm afraid we left your car there, Dad,' she told him shakily.

'She was in no state to drive,' Bill put in.

Andrew frowned, puzzled, and looked at the other man.

'What were you doing there, Bill?'

Bill quickly explained how he had seen Margaret drive past the pub and how he had followed.

'Thank goodness I did!' he added, speaking directly to Margaret. 'Your parents might never have seen either of you again!'

As Mrs Harris returned at that moment, Margaret bit back her angry retort.

Bill sat down, making it clear he had no intention of leaving.

'Angie's exhausted,' Mrs Harris told them. 'The poor girl . . . '

'At least she's safe,' her husband said calmly.

He looked startled when she rounded on him, her eyes wide, her lips tight.

'Yes, but no thanks to you!' she snapped.

He frowned, looking puzzled.

'Yes, you!' she qualified furiously. 'You've always been far too indulgent! When Margaret showed you that wretched disk, you should have gone straight to the police, but oh no! Not you!'

'At the time, it didn't seem the right thing to do,' he replied. 'With hindsight maybe . . . '

But Mrs Harris wasn't interested in hindsight.

'Goodness knows how this will affect Angie! Have you any idea what she's been through?'

Margaret had never known her parents quarrel like this. They had arguments, of course — everyone did — but this was different.

'Angie isn't a little girl any more!' her father snapped. 'She'll get over it. If you didn't smother her . . . '

160

'Smother her!'

'Mum — Dad — please,' Margaret begged. 'Don't! You're going to say something you'll regret. It isn't worth it. It's over . . . It's over.'

Bill reached out and took her hand. The gesture was at once reassuring and filled with warmth.

Andrew Harris looked shocked, as if he couldn't quite understand his own behaviour. His wife just looked plain hurt.

'Margaret's right,' he said at length. 'And we're all tired. Let's sleep on it and talk again in the morning.'

Margaret took her father's cue and got to her feet. Bill remained seated.

'I'm not going anywhere — ' he said softly ' — without an explanation. I think you owe me that, Margaret.'

She nodded to her parents, kissed them both goodnight, then closed the kitchen door behind them.

★ ★ ★

'Well?' Bill prompted, his tone surprisingly tender.

Margaret sank down on to a chair and tried to explain, but nothing she said made any sense. She gabbled about new partners and deals with Middle Eastern banks . . . and about illegal exports that Jack hadn't known about. And about the computer disk that could have proved it — if they'd been able to read it . . .

Her voice lowered and her hands shook. Obviously, despite her assurances to the contrary, she was still far from all right. And putting pressure on her to explain wasn't helping.

He smiled tenderly and touched her face. Her skin felt hot despite the lack of colour.

'You're not making a lot of sense, love,' he said. 'Let's leave it for tonight. Will you be at work tomorrow? Silly question, of course you will. We'll go somewhere quiet for lunch and have a proper talk. Will I pick you up about one?'

Margaret was grateful and, as he went to leave by the back door, she slipped her arms around his waist, resting her head against his chest.

'Thanks for being there,' she murmured. 'I know I said some rotten things, but I'm glad you turned up when you did.'

'So am I,' he whispered.

He lowered his head and kissed her goodnight. Then he was gone, hurrying off into the darkness.

Margaret frowned as she closed the door. The kiss had been lacking something, what she wasn't sure. It was almost as if it had been dutiful rather than loving . . .

She slid the bolts across, checked the windows, then went round the other rooms. Jack's enemies had got what they wanted but she still needed to feel safe.

The noise in the kitchen stopped her in her tracks. For a moment she was too terrified to move, then she heard the familiar off-key whistle . . .

Opening the door, she found Ben rummaging in the fridge.

'Caught in the act!' He grinned sheepishly. 'What are you doing down here at this time of night? Couldn't sleep?'

Ben . . . with his hair all tousled and his pyjamas crumpled . . . Margaret smiled. She hadn't realised how much her family meant to her before now. Or how lucky she was to have them . . .

She looked pointedly at his piled plate.

'Sure you've got enough there?'

He grinned.

'I'm starving! That boyfriend of yours is a real slave-driver. But I'm enjoying every minute of it.'

She watched as he poured a glass of milk.

'Did I hear Mum and Dad arguing earlier?' He frowned. 'I don't know what Dad's done, but he's really upset her.'

Margaret didn't really want to talk about their parents. And they'd agreed not to tell Ben what was going on.

'Do you think you might stay with Bill?' she asked, changing the subject back.

'I'd like to. I know it's not the career I wanted, but I'm happy doing it and we get along well. That's the important thing, isn't it? I mean, that's why you went to work for Jack Stanton, isn't it?'

Margaret nodded. He looked so eager, so full of enthusiasm. At any other time, she would have been so happy for him, but right now she had too much on her mind.

'Bill's great,' he went on as he sat himself down at the table. 'He's been part of this family so long, I almost think of him as a brother. You're not going to let him get away, are you, Mags?'

Margaret simply shook her head. How could she answer a question like that when she didn't know herself?

'Night, Ben.' She ruffled his untidy hair. 'Sleep tight.'

He grinned up at her cheerfully.

'Don't let the bed bugs bite!'

And despite all that had happened — all that could still happen — Margaret left the room with a smile on her face . . .

Another Woman

Margaret found it difficult to concentrate the following day. Still, it was good to be able to lose herself in her work for a while.

'Just autograph these, will you?' Louise bustled in with a pile of letters. 'I want to catch the lunch-time post with them.'

'That was quick!' Margaret smiled as she began signing.

They were all requests to people to pay their accounts. With Jack away, she was trying to gather in as much money as possible to keep things ticking over.

As the police investigation progressed, the office staff were gradually being allowed access to more files and equipment, although it would be a long time before they were back at full strength.

'I'll be going out for lunch about

one,' she told Louise. 'I may be a little late back.'

She had mixed feelings about this lunch date with Bill. She was looking forward to it, but at the same time she felt a sense of trepidation.

'Where are we going?' she asked as he opened the door of the Land-Rover for her.

'It's such a lovely day, I've packed us a picnic,' he said cheerfully. 'You don't mind, do you?'

'Of course not.'

Bill drove out of Stanford and, as grey buildings gave way to green hills, Margaret felt some of the tension ease out of her. They talked about the weather and other mundane matters, almost as if they were strangers.

At last he pulled up in a parking space and they walked a little way to find just the right spot where they spread a large plaid rug on the grass.

The view was wonderful, spread out before her like a tapestry. So many shades of green and gold and brown

. . . capped by a flawless blue sky . . .

For the next hour, Bill didn't once mention Jack, and as they talked of normal, everyday things, Margaret began to relax.

Bill chuckled. 'I've left Ben putting up a shed for the donkeys!'

Margaret found herself laughing, too.

'That's the idea — keep him busy. It'll keep him out of mischief, too.'

Bill stopped laughing and gazed at her.

'And what about you, Margaret? What do I have to do to keep you out of mischief?'

She drew in her breath. The time had come to tell him everything.

Haltingly she explained all that had happened, from the moment Jack had arrived at her flat late one night . . .

When she'd finished, he stared at her.

'And you trust him? You think he's telling you the truth?'

'Yes. I . . . I can't explain why, but I just know Jack's innocent. I know you don't like him very much, but he's a decent man.'

She spoke with such vehemence, such belief, that Bill fell silent for along time.

When at last he turned to look at her again, there was such sadness in his eyes, it made her catch her breath.

'Just what is Jack Stanton to you?' he asked her quietly.

It was the question she had been dreading . . .

As her silence continued, Bill drew in his breath.

'Are you in love with him?'

She wanted to cry out a denial, but she couldn't speak. Tears choked her. How could she explain how she felt when she didn't know herself?

'I don't know,' she breathed at last. 'I'm sorry, but I'm so mixed up, I don't know how I feel about anything — or anyone.'

He let out his breath and looked relieved that she at least hadn't given him the one answer he didn't want to hear.

'Can you be patient with me, Bill?'

she went on. 'Wait until all this trouble is sorted out? I know I'm asking a lot . . . '

He thought for a moment, then nodded. Really, he had no choice.

Margaret watched as he began to pack their picnic things away. Poor Bill . . .

'Bill, I . . . '

'I have to go up north for a few days,' he cut in, his voice cool and business-like. 'There's an auction I should go to. I've seen the catalogue and there's some stuff that would suit the museum. I could take Ben . . . '

'He'd love that!'

'I know. But I hate going at a time like this.'

'Of course you must go!' she insisted. 'It won't be for long, will it?'

It would give them both a breathing space. Time to reflect and consider their relationship . . .

★ ★ ★

When Margaret returned to the office, Louise handed her a pile of phone messages.

'A woman keeps calling and asking for you. She won't leave a message.'

'Sounds ominous! Did she leave a name?'

'No. She just said she would try again.'

Within five minutes of Margaret sitting down at her desk, the phone buzzed.

'It's the mystery woman on the line,' Louise told her. 'I'll put her through.'

'Hello?' Margaret hoped she sounded more confident than she felt. 'This is Margaret Harris speaking.'

'At last! Thank goodness!' The voice spoke in a hurried whisper. 'Look — you don't know me — my name is Susannah Robinson.'

Susannah? Wasn't that the name of the woman in the photograph in Jack's room?

'Is there any news of Jack?' Susannah demanded. 'I've been worried sick. I kept putting off calling you, hoping he would get in touch — but he hasn't.' She sounded genuinely distressed.

Margaret knew she had to be careful what she said.

'I really can't . . . ' she began.

'Look, I know he trusted you more than anyone,' Susannah broke in. 'He told me he didn't know what he would do without you.'

Margaret felt flattered — but confused. How did Susannah know so much about her when she knew nothing about Susannah?

'Could we meet?' Susannah suggested.

'That's not a bad idea,' Margaret agreed, curious to find out more about this woman who meant so much to Jack.

'I'm a member of the Stanford Sports Centre,' Susannah was saying. 'Could we meet there in — say, an hour? It's 'members only' this afternoon, so it'll be quiet. I'll tell Gordon I've arranged a game of squash . . . '

'Gordon?'

'My husband.' Susannah lowered her voice. 'I've a feeling he knows more . . .' She broke off. 'That's him now! I'll have to go. I'll see you in an hour.'

★　★　★

Margaret's first impression was that Susannah was even more beautiful than her photograph. And nervous.

They introduced themselves and Susannah stood twisting her wedding ring round and round on her finger.

Once she had signed them in, she led the way to the coffee bar, walking with an easy grace that Margaret envied. She looked elegant, even in tracksuit and trainers.

'Shall we sit over there by the window?' she suggested.

They ordered a pot of coffee and chatted quite comfortably together while they waited for the waitress to bring it over. Margaret felt quite at ease with Susannah. Was it because they had their mutual concern for Jack in common?

'I hope you didn't mind me calling you,' Susannah said. 'It's just, I've known Jack for years — and I know he's innocent.'

Margaret sighed. 'I wish everyone had your faith!' She eyed the other girl. 'So, why did you want to meet me?'

'I'm desperate to know what's happening. There's no-one I can talk to — certainly not Gordon!' Susannah paused and took a deep breath. 'You see, I think he has something to do with all this. I know Jack was having some sort of cash flow problem . . . and Gordon put him in touch with these bankers. Apparently they were willing to invest in his company.'

So that's how Jack had got involved, Margaret thought. Through a friend. Yet she'd never even heard of Gordon Robinson . . .

'He kept it all very quiet,' she told Susannah. 'But then, that's Jack's way. He likes to keep a lid on things until they're settled.'

Susannah nodded, as if she knew that very well. She poured out two cups of coffee and passed one over.

'Jack was uneasy about it,' she went on. 'But Gordon assured him it was all above board. Now I'm not so sure.'

'You said you've known Jack for years,' Margaret prompted. She had to be sure that Susannah was a genuine friend . . .

'Through Gordon actually.' Colour flooded the other woman's cheeks and she wouldn't meet Margaret's gaze.

'They went to school together and occasionally did business,' she continued in a rush. 'I met Jack for the first time at our wedding. If only it had been before . . . ' She broke off and bit her lip.

Margaret said nothing. She wasn't here to judge. Just to listen.

'Jack and I have been . . . close, for some time now. He came on holiday with us to our villa in Spain. Gordon, as usual, was tied up with his work and left me to myself much of the time. Jack

176

took pity on me.

'One day we drove into the mountains.' Her eyes sparkled as she remembered. 'We stopped at this little village and had lunch. On the veranda of the hotel, you felt as if you were at the top of the world!

'Jack made me laugh. Something I hadn't done for a long time . . . ' Her voice was tight as if she expected Margaret to condemn her.

'You don't have to tell me all this,' Margaret protested softly, but it was obvious Susannah needed to talk.

'While we were there, there was a fire in the hotel. The owner's little boy was trapped inside. He was only four . . . Jack went rushing into the black smoke. I'll never forget seeing him come staggering out, the little boy unconscious in his arms . . . '

Both women were silent for a long time; Susannah was remembering, while Margaret was learning more about Jack.

Susannah's unexpected laughter brought

her back down to earth.

'The owner of the little hotel was so grateful! He swore eternal friendship . . . He thought we were a couple, blessed us both and invited us to stay at his hotel any time!

'We never told anyone what happened that day. Not even Gordon. It was ours you see, Jack's and mine. Jack always said he'd like to go back . . . '

She looked up, her eyes misting, and Margaret realised that she used to be — and still was — in love with Jack. But — what about her husband?

The question must have been obvious in her eyes.

'Gordon married me because he needed a wife,' Susannah explained. 'Someone decorative to help his career . . . to organise his home . . . to act as hostess at his dinner parties. And I'm very good at all that!

'Don't look so shocked, Margaret! Not all marriages are made in heaven.'

'But why stay married to him when

you don't love him — when you love someone else?'

'Loyalty? It's a very affluent life — and I admit I enjoy it. But then I met Jack, and realised what was lacking ... what I'd never have with Gordon. He'd never have dreamed of rushing into a burning building to rescue a little boy he didn't even know. Everything has to be precise and organised with Gordon; there's no way he would act on impulse.

'Jack and I ... we meet for dinner now and again. That's as far as it goes — as far as it ever will go.'

Reaching into her bag, Susannah pulled out some tissues and dabbed at her eyes.

'I'll give you my number,' she said when she had pulled herself together. 'Will you let me know if you hear anything — please? And if there's anything I can do — anything at all — don't hesitate to get in touch.'

'I will.' Margaret's heart went out to her. 'But I must go now. I've so much to do at work . . . '

'I understand.'

However, despite her promises to keep in touch, Margaret wasn't sure if she should. Could she really trust Susannah Robinson?

She had thought she knew Jack pretty well, but she had never guessed there was a side like this to him. It made her wonder what else she didn't know . . .

★   ★   ★

The following day Margaret went to see Barbara Stanton again. To her relief, the woman was up and about again, apparently fully recovered from her angina attack.

Margaret hoped Jack would call when she was there. She had timed it deliberately. She had to let him know what had happened to the disk.

It was just as she was preparing to leave that Edith rushed round from next-door to tell them there was a call.

'You go ahead, dear,' Barbara Stanton urged Margaret. 'It takes me ages to get through.'

Margaret ran next door and picked up the phone.

'Jack?' she said urgently. 'They've got the disk!'

There was a stunned silence at the other end of the line while he digested this.

'I don't suppose you handed it over willingly,' he said finally. 'You weren't hurt, were you?'

'No, but they kidnapped Angie. I had no choice, Jack. They tested the disk on a lap-top. And they asked me for the copy. Is there a copy, Jack?'

He laughed bitterly. 'Sadly not. I didn't have time to make one.'

There was so much she wanted to tell him but she could hear Barbara Stanton and Edith coming and she was running out of time.

'There's more. Angie overheard them talking. They know where you are . . . '

'It's all right. Don't worry about me

— I can look after myself. Angie wasn't hurt?'

'No, thank God. Just frightened.'

'Thank goodness. I'm sorry. If I'd known it would involve your family, I'd never have given you the thing!'

There was a faint stir at his end of the line and she heard him murmur, 'Gracias, Luis,' then a foreign voice replied, 'No hay de que.'

She strained to hear as more voices joined in, but it was too much of a distant babble to make out any words.

'Jack?'

He didn't reply. She could almost feel his tension down the line.

Mrs Stanton was standing beside her now and Margaret tried not to let her anxiety show.

'Your mother's here, Jack.'

'Give her my love,' he said quickly, his voice low. 'I have to go.'

With that he hung up.

Margaret looked at the phone. She hadn't had a chance to tell him about her meeting with Susannah.

'I'm sorry.' She turned to Mrs Stanton. 'He had to go.'

The woman looked disappointed, but shrugged.

'Well, thank you for coming, dear. I do appreciate your visits — and all you're doing for Jack.'

Impulsively Margaret ducked to kiss Barbara Stanton on the cheek. Then she said goodbye and hurried out to her car.

Talking to Jack had upset her. She drove down the road a little way, then pulled in at a quiet spot, wondering what the detective following her would make of her behaviour. Well, she didn't care!

Her head was spinning and she didn't know what to do next.

She had caused trouble between her parents, and Angie had been put through a terrifying ordeal. And she and Bill were on the point of splitting up . . .

It was all becoming more than she could bear. To her horror, she burst into tears.

DC Ken Watkins had pulled in behind her and he came to tap on the window, his face a picture of concern.

'Is everything all right, Miss Harris?'

Nodding, she grabbed a handful of tissues from the glove compartment. The young detective paused, embarrassed, then walked back to his car.

With the tissues had come the piece of paper with Susannah's telephone number. Margaret stared at it.

Of course! That was it! It had been staring her in the face all the time . . .

★ ★ ★

Jack quietly put the phone down and pressed himself into the alcove. The four men who had just walked into the hotel lobby didn't look as if they belonged to this quiet little village.

He watched as the hotel manager argued with them, trying to understand what was being said, but the only words he recognised were his own name.

After what seemed an age, they

turned and left, obviously displeased.

Jack closed his eyes in relief.

He opened them to find himself face to face with the manager, grinning all over his face.

'They won't come back, Señor Stanton.'

'I'm sorry, Luis.' Jack's voice was grim. 'I never intended to bring trouble here.'

'It is no matter.' Luis shook his head. 'You are always welcome here.'

Jack looked up and saw a skinny little boy peeping at him around the corner. He'd grown taller and his black curly hair was shorter, but Jack recognised the impish grin he'd last seen in a hospital ward.

For a moment, he could see that same boy sprawled in the hotel kitchen surrounded by black smoke and leaping flames . . .

He had already put one family in danger; he couldn't do it to another.

'I can't stay here,' he declared. 'I should never have come in the first place.'

'Stay for tonight,' Luis insisted. 'Those men will not come back. Why should they? And you look as if you need a rest.'

'No, Luis, I . . . '

'I have never forgotten what you did for Rafael. I owe you his life. Please let me repay you.'

'You don't understand,' Jack mumbled. 'It's too dangerous . . . '

Jack, At Last!

Jack was still at the hotel the following afternoon. He had finally allowed himself to believe that Luis was right, that the men wouldn't look for him again there.

It was so good to stop running, to feel safe even for just a few hours . . .

Then Rafael came rushing in, spilling out a stream of Spanish. Luis rushed to the window that overlooked the street.

Jack got hurriedly to his feet.

'What is it?'

'A woman in the village. She's asking directions here,' Luis told him. 'It may only be a tourist . . . '

Jack joined Luis at the window and felt his stomach lurch as a hire car pulled up outside the hotel. He watched as a woman climbed from the car, her eyes hidden behind dark sunglasses. She was slim and smartly dressed, with a wide-brimmed straw hat protecting her from the sun.

As she turned towards the hotel, hesitating as though plucking up the courage to come in, Jack let out a shout and rushed to the door. His feet pounded down the steps and then he was face to face with her.

'Jack!' She stepped back to look up at him, the nervousness gone.

He opened his arms and she was in them and he held her as if he would never let her go. She hugged him back, as pleased to see him safe and sound as he was to see her.

'Oh, Jack, I'm so glad I found you!'

'So am I.' He grinned, holding her at arm's length so he could have a proper look at her. 'But what on earth are you doing here? How did you know where I was?'

'Oh, Jack . . . ' To her dismay, she could feel tears welling in her eyes. She had known she would be relieved to find him safe and well but she had never imagined she would be so pleased just to see him. And what about *his* reaction?

His joy seemed so spontaneous and so genuine, it touched something deep inside her.

They were still standing outside the hotel at the bottom of the steps, but it could have been anywhere in the world for all she cared. Right now nothing else mattered except Jack.

'Hey!' He gently tilted her chin, his blue eyes searching hers. 'It's all right, love.'

For one heart-stopping moment, she thought he would hug her again. That wouldn't be so dreadful . . . except for the way it made her feel. On the one hand it seemed so strange, so wrong . . . On the other . . .

'You look wonderful,' he said gruffly.

She felt herself blushing at the unexpected compliment. He's just glad to see a familiar face, she told herself firmly.

'Let's get out of here,' he went on. 'Would you like to stretch your legs a bit?'

She nodded, too choked to speak. She was feeling cramped from the journey and a walk and some fresh air might be what she needed to get her thoughts in order.

Jack stooped to pick up her straw hat which had been knocked to the ground in the commotion.

With a smile, he put it back on her head.

'We don't want you coming down with heatstroke!'

She managed a small smile in reply.

They walked slowly side by side along the village street.

'You shouldn't have come!' he said urgently and she flinched at the harshness of his words.

Suddenly they might as well have been miles apart. She felt cold despite the sun. The closeness she had felt earlier had evaporated.

'I had to!' she cried.

He turned to look at her, and his expression softened.

'Don't get me wrong. It's wonderful

to see you — but it might not be safe.'

As he took her arm, her breath caught in her throat at his touch. Jack's eyes flew to hers — and what she saw there made her heart leap.

Then he dropped his hand and the distance between them seemed greater than ever. It hurt more than she thought possible.

'So how did you find me?' he asked at last. His voice wasn't quite steady.

'Susannah.'

'Susannah?' he echoed in a whisper. For a long moment he was deep in thought. What was he remembering?

'How is she?' he asked at last.

'Unhappy,' she replied truthfully. 'I think she's in love with you, Jack. How — how do you feel about her?'

She had to know. It was none of her business, but she had to know.

'Susannah's very special to me,' he replied guardedly. 'I care for her, but I'm not in love with her.' He sighed. 'For a while I thought I was — but you can love someone without being *in* love

191

with them. Do you know what I mean?'

She nodded slowly. Didn't that describe how she felt about Bill? She loved him and cared for him, but there were no fireworks, no flashing lights . . .

'What did she tell you?' he asked, jolting her back to reality.

'Actually she thinks her husband may be involved. She thinks you may have been set up from the start.'

He looked at her, and for a moment his steps slowed.

'But Gordon and I have been friends for years. I can't believe he would do that to me — and yet . . . ' He frowned, as if struggling to come to terms with the truth. 'I've always wondered about his involvement in all this. But what would he gain if Stanton's went under? If I . . . '

'There's a lot of money to be made illegally, in all kinds of dodgy deals,' Margaret said softly. 'And a lot to lose if you're caught. Fines, prison sentences . . . The disk might not only prove your innocence, it might also show who's responsible.'

Jack sighed. 'That's what's been worrying me all along. Who I might be involving.'

After a moment, he went on: 'Did Susannah say anything else?'

'She told me about how you saved a little boy's life . . .'

'No, no! About Gordon.' He sounded impatient.

'Just that she thinks he's involved.' She thought for a moment. 'I suppose if he knew about you and Susannah . . .'

He turned to face her and gently took both her hands in his.

'There's nothing to know!' he said insistently.

Margaret shivered at his touch. I'm tired and frightened, she told herself. No wonder I'm so confused! But hadn't she always felt a little like this when she was with Jack? Hadn't Bill been able to see it, even if she hadn't?

Jack released her hands. 'Let's get back to the hotel. I'll ask Luis to make us some coffee.'

It was cool inside the hotel. And quiet, apart from the swish of the ceiling fans.

Margaret had been inordinately pleased to hear Jack wasn't in love with Susannah. Why? She wasn't free herself; there was Bill. And even if she was . . . Well, Jack wouldn't be interested in her — would he?

To cover her confusion, she chattered on about his mother.

'You've become very fond of her, haven't you?' he observed with a smile at last.

'She's a lovely lady,' she acknowledged. 'And she's done nothing to deserve all this worry!'

'I suppose I deserved that.' He sounded rueful. 'You do understand why I had to get away though, don't you, Margaret? I would never have stood a chance of proving my innocence if I was locked up. I hardly dare ask — how's the business? Do I still *have* a business?'

'We're gradually getting back to

something approaching normal.' She smiled happily at him. 'Louise has been great. I don't think I could have coped without her.'

She stopped. Jack was looking despondent.

'What does it matter?' he sighed. 'It's all over anyway, without that disk. Imagine — your whole life depending on something so small . . .'

But Margaret wasn't listening. She was rummaging in her bag while Jack watched, bemused.

'My father knows a bit about computers,' she was saying rather vaguely. 'We tried to read the disk — ah, got it!' Her fingers closed over what she was looking for.

'What are you saying, Margaret?' Jack was laughing. 'He surely didn't crack the password?'

'Not in a million years. But he managed to copy the disk!' Triumphantly she put an envelope on the table between them. 'The information is there, Jack. It still exists!'

Jack stared at it in disbelief for several seconds. Then he reached out almost tentatively and picked it up.

'Your father is a very smart man,' he said appreciatively. 'Now all I need is that password! If I can find the information I need, perhaps I can even protect Gordon . . .'

Margaret smiled proudly. 'That's why I came to Spain.'

'I'd kiss you — ' Jack grinned wickedly ' — but I know you're mad about Bill. How is he, by the way?'

She was caught unawares by a sudden rush of guilt.

'He's fine,' she said steadily.

'And the family?'

'They're all OK.'

But her smile wavered when she thought of her father back home. He was going to have a lot of explaining to do . . .

★ ★ ★

I'll get it!' Jenny Harris hurried to answer the telephone, smiling when she heard Bill's voice.

'I'd have thought you'd be too busy with your auctions and things to call us!' she teased.

'Ah, you know me — I've always got time for my lady love! Is Margaret there?' he asked. 'Could I have a quick word?'

'No — she's not here,' she faltered uncertainly, and Andrew looked up from behind his newspaper as he overheard. 'She's with you — isn't she?'

Her legs suddenly weak, she sank down on to a chair. If Margaret wasn't with Bill — then where was she? It was all starting again, this awful nightmare!

'She's not with me.' Bill's voice was sharp with fear.

'Have you tried her flat?' Jenny suggested. 'Or the office?'

'I've already tried both, and her mobile is switched off,' he told her. 'You were my last hope.'

'I don't believe this . . . ' Her voice was a whisper.

'Look — I'm coming back straight

away.' Bill told her firmly. 'Goodness knows what she's got herself into now!'

She felt the sudden warm weight of Andrew's hand on her shoulder. He had come to stand beside her.

'It's Margaret,' she told him. 'Bill doesn't know where she is!'

'I'll be there in a few hours,' Bill said, and hung up.

As she put the phone down with trembling hands, Andrew squeezed her shoulder in an attempt to comfort her.

'Don't worry,' he murmured.

'Don't worry?' she echoed in disbelief. 'How can I help but worry? First Angie, now Margaret. Where's it going to end? I thought she'd gone with Bill . . . Where is she, Andrew? What's happened to her?'

He could only shrug helplessly and she stared at him. How could he be so calm, so unruffled? Unless . . . He was refusing to meet her gaze, she noticed.

'You know, don't you?' she whispered incredulously. 'You know where she is. Where is she, Andrew? Have those men got her? Like Angie?'

'It's nothing like that,' he replied quickly. 'She's quite safe.'

'Then where is she?'

He looked away, shaking his head. 'I can't tell you.'

'What do you mean?'

'Please — don't ask me, Jenny. Just trust me.'

'Trust you!'

She felt so angry, so betrayed . . . and she was struggling to find the words to tell him so when Angie came into the room.

She stopped abruptly as soon as she realised that she had walked into the middle of a row. Her cheerful smile faded and she looked from one parent to the other in bewilderment. They rarely argued — not like this anyway.

'What's happening?' she asked nervously.

'Ask your father!' Jenny snapped and stormed out, her feet banging on every step as she ran upstairs.

Angie turned to look at him.

'Dad . . . ?'

When he didn't answer, she made to follow her mother, but he laid his hand on her arm to stop her.

'Leave her,' he said softly.

She looked at him, puzzled.

'What's going on, Dad? I've never seen Mum so upset.'

'It's Margaret. She's gone away — but I promised I wouldn't tell anyone where. I hoped she'd be back before anyone realised she's not been around. Darn it, if only Bill hadn't called . . . '

'Margaret's not with him then?' Angie sat down. 'I thought . . . '

'That's what you were all meant to think,' he admitted. 'That they'd made a last-minute decision to go off for a few days together.'

There was a crash from upstairs and they both flinched and looked upwards. She gave him a sympathetic smile.

'You'd better go and talk to Mum,' she said. 'I'll make some tea.'

He kissed the top of her head. 'Good girl.'

His wife was at the linen cupboard door with a pile of bedding in her arms when he reached the top of the stairs.

'What in the world are you doing, Jen?'

'What does it look like?' she snapped. 'I'm moving into the spare room!'

'Jen, please — don't do anything hasty,' he pleaded. 'We can sort this out.'

She gave him a hostile stare.

'You know where she is, don't you? And you won't tell me!'

'I can't. I promised.'

'For goodness sake, Andrew, I'm your wife! Margaret's mother,' she exploded. 'Can't *you* trust *me*? What do you think I'm going to do? Go running to the police? The papers?' She paused and took a deep breath.

'Not only am I worried sick, but now I'm shut out, too. Do you have any idea how much you've hurt me? First about that wretched disk and now . . . '

She broke off and squeezed her eyes

shut. Now, no matter how much Andrew insisted Margaret was all right, Jenny couldn't be sure it was the truth.

She'd spent most of her life with this man. Loved and respected him above all others. Now she felt he just wasn't who she had thought he was.

'I'm not shutting you out.' He put his hands on her shoulders. 'I'm trying to protect you!'

She wrenched herself away.

'That's not how it feels.'

'Listen!' he begged. 'Let me explain.'

Her shoulders seemed to sag as she looked at him, and at last she noticed that he seemed as exhausted and worried as she felt.

'Where is she?' she asked him again, more calmly now.

He shook his head. 'I can't . . .'

With a cry of exasperation, she pushed past him and into the spare room where she threw the bedding down in a heap.

She tried to straighten the duvet, but it was twisted inside the cover and, no matter how she shook it, it wouldn't lie flat. Tears of frustration sprang to her eyes.

Gently Andrew moved her to one side and methodically straightened the duvet and cover until it was lying flat on the bed.

'There,' he said, with the suggestion of a smile.

She drew in her breath, looked up at him and their eyes met. Perhaps she felt so betrayed because she loved him so much . . .

'I was afraid to tell you,' he confessed and, as she turned to move away, he reached out and took her arm, making her stop and listen.

'Margaret and I agreed it would be better if no-one else knew. We didn't want you to worry, and for this to work, we had to be sure everyone would behave normally.'

'You didn't trust me,' she whispered. 'I can't forgive you for that, Andrew.'

'I couldn't take the risk. You've been through so much . . . '

She closed her eyes and sat down on

the bed. She wanted to feel his arms around her. She wanted him to tell her everything was all right . . . but if he came anywhere near her, she would probably kick him. Hard!

Torn between anger and grief, she looked up at him through a haze of tears.

'Is she really all right? Are you telling me the truth about that?'

'Yes, Jenny, I swear.'

She looked at him levelly.

'For your sake — and for the sake of our marriage — I hope so.'

They both jumped when the doorbell rang.

'I'll get it!' Angie's voice drifted up the stairs.

Minutes later there was a tap on the bedroom door and Angie poked her head into the room.

'It's the police. They want to talk to you.'

Andrew and Jenny exchanged an anxious glance.

'We'll be right down,' he said calmly. 'Perhaps you could make them a cup of tea?'

'Right-oh!' Angie hurried downstairs.

'They'll have realised she's given them the slip,' Andrew said softly. 'We'll say we've only just found out ourselves that she isn't with Bill . . . that's why you've been crying.'

Jenny's hand flew to her face as she glanced in the mirror. The reflection that looked back was tear-stained and haggard.

Andrew's smile was gentle and he held out his hand to her.

'Come on, love, we can do it,' he urged.

Haltingly she took a step towards him, then another, and then she placed her hand in his. His fingers closed around it and she felt his strength. At least she wouldn't have to pretend to be worried. Her concern was painfully real.

'Ready?' he whispered, giving her hand a squeeze.

She nodded. They had to present a united front, she told herself. But that didn't mean she had forgiven him!

No End To The Nightmare

Margaret was sitting alone at a table, gazing thoughtfully into space.

'Good afternoon,' said the small, clear voice of a child.

She turned and saw a little black-haired boy and smiled. He gave a small bow and when he straightened, his smile was perfectly white — except for two dark gaps in the front where he was missing teeth.

'Good afternoon,' Margaret replied.

'I am Rafael,' he continued carefully. 'My father says I am to prac . . . prac . . .'

He broke off, pressed his finger into his chin and looked towards the ceiling for inspiration.

'Practise,' Margaret whispered.

'Practise,' he parroted, then again just to be sure. 'Practise. He say I am to practise my English.'

Margaret laughed.

'Let me tell you, young man, your English is much better than my Spanish. Won't you sit down, Rafael?'

So this was the child Jack had rescued from the fire. Well, she would be glad of the company.

Jack had left the hotel before she was even awake. His note had simply said he had some business to attend to and that he would be back later.

Luis came over to the table with a pot of coffee and looked sternly at his son.

'You are not bothering the señorita I hope, Rafael?'

'He's not bothering me,' Margaret said quickly. 'In fact I was hoping he might like to come with me for a walk.' She felt it would be nice to get outdoors and make the most of the glorious sunshine.

Outside, there was a light breeze coming down from the mountains. It relieved the heat a little, making the day altogether more pleasant.

It never occurred to Margaret that it wouldn't be safe to walk in the quiet streets. The village was such a peaceful place, not a favourite of tourists . . .

They chatted as they walked, Rafael in his version of English, Margaret helping him out now and then . . .

She suddenly realised the little boy had fallen silent and was looking around, alert and wary.

'What is it?' she asked.

'Car coming. I wonder who it is?'

He was aware that Jack and his father were very suspicious of any cars appearing in the village at the moment.

They stood in the shadows of a large white building in the village square. A fountain played in the centre and for a moment Margaret was mesmerised by the sunlight dancing through the water.

A hire car drove slowly into the square, pulling up on the forecourt of the garage opposite.

Margaret watched as the driver got out and stood beside the car, looking all around. He wore a panama hat, which he tipped to the back of his head. As if it would help him to see more. What was he looking for?

'Señorita . . . Señorita . . . ' Rafael pulled at her hand. 'We go, we go.'

The man took off his sunglasses and looked around again. This time he stopped when he saw Margaret.

Despite the warmth of the sun, she shivered. Even across the square, she saw recognition dawn and, at the same time, she realised that he looked vaguely familiar to her.

It was as though she was mesmerised. She couldn't move.

The man put his sunglasses back on and took a step or two towards her, breaking the spell.

Gripping Rafael's hand, Margaret turned away from the hotel. The little boy resisted, trying to pull her back the way they had come.

'No, Señorita,' he whispered. 'This way!'

They turned into a dark alley. Then, hand in hand, they ran.

Rafael led her through a bewildering network of back alleys, yet still she kept expecting the man to appear behind them. However, when they finally stopped, high up the hill behind the village, no-one was following.

It was a wonderful vantage point. The village square could be seen quite clearly. The stranger was still there, standing beside his car while a young man filled it with petrol.

He was looking around while he waited ... looking for her? It was a chilling thought.

Margaret sat down on a rock. There was grit in her sandals and her feet hurt, but that was the least of her worries.

Where had see seen him before? It was such a vague recollection ... and Jack had brought so many people to the office.

She saw the man pay for his petrol then climb into his car and drive off in the direction from which he had come.

She smiled at Rafael.

'Come on. Let's get back.'

This time, they walked slowly.

'Do you know who he was?' she asked the boy 'The man in the car?'

'He comes sometimes.' Rafael shrugged. 'I do not know his name.'

Margaret hadn't realised how long she'd been gone until she saw Jack's worried face. He stood at the top of the hotel steps watching them come along the street.

'Where have you been? What were you thinking of? Wandering off on your own like that?'

Rafael slipped away and Margaret suddenly felt like crying.

'I saw a man . . . I don't know . . . he looked familiar,' she stammered. 'He stared at me as if he knew me . . .'

Jack saw the fear in her face and his anger dissolved. He came down the steps towards her.

'I've been so worried.' His voice was no longer harsh.

Then she was in his arms, clinging to him as he held her tight against him.

'I was so scared,' she sobbed.

'Me, too,' he admitted. 'If anything happened to you, I don't know what I'd do.'

They pulled apart slightly. She held her breath as their eyes met and the true meaning of his words began to sink in for both of them. She still couldn't quite believe it as his lips came down to meet hers . . .

She had never been kissed like that before. Certainly not by Bill. If she had, she would never have let him out of her sight!

'If only you knew how long I've wanted to do that,' Jack whispered as they finally pulled apart.

Margaret was flushed, confused, her mind reeling. Did he mean it? Or was the tension playing havoc with their emotions?

He leaned forward again, but this time his lips only brushed her forehead. She felt ridiculously disappointed.

'Which way did he go?' he asked.

'Who?' she asked, momentarily disorientated. 'Oh, the man . . . that way, I think.' She pointed vaguely. 'Back down the mountain. The way he'd come.'

'OK. You go back inside. Have a drink. I'll go and ask around. See if anyone knows him.'

With that, he was gone, and Margaret was left standing alone on the steps, her mind in a whirl.

★   ★   ★

What seemed like hours later, Margaret stood by the window, staring out at the darkening street. It was so peaceful and quiet out there, but she was having to fight her growing unease. What if something had happened to Jack? What should she do?

'It has been a long day for you, Señorita,' Luis said behind her. 'Why don't you go to bed now? I will wake you as soon as Jack returns.'

She shook her head. 'Thanks, Luis, but I'd rather wait.'

'Then I will make some more coffee,' Luis offered and headed towards the kitchens.

The night had grown cool. The mountains looked dark and forbidding. Margaret shivered. She was so far from home, from her parents — and Bill.

Outside it was almost complete darkness. She moved away from the window and sank into a chair. She was exhausted, but she couldn't even think of going to bed until Jack came back.

If Jack came back! What if he didn't? What would she do then?'

She had thought the nightmare was nearly over, but it wasn't. Perhaps it never would be.

Restlessly she got up and went to the window again. There was nothing to see outside now but her own reflection in the glass, etched against the inky darkness outside.

She choked back a sob. It was no use going to pieces. Jack needed her more than ever. But what about Bill? Didn't he need her, too? He'd said so often enough. And told her he loved her. But did Jack? *Really* love her?

Certainly Jack's kiss had made her senses reel in a way Bill's never had. Goodness, if she'd felt like that she would have married him long ago!

But perhaps she wasn't being realistic. The situation with Jack was extraordinary. If Bill was in trouble, wouldn't that make a difference? Heighten the feelings she had towards him?

She wasn't sure. She wasn't sure about anything any more.

'Please come back,' she whispered.

But the darkness outside remained still and silent. No-one came near the hotel.

It wasn't just a question of what to do if Jack didn't come back, she realised suddenly. She had to ask herself what she would do if he did.

What would she do about Bill?

★   ★   ★

It was almost dawn before she finally fell asleep. Even then it was only a

215

troubled and restless doze.

The sun was streaming in through the half-open blind when the ringing of the phone jerked her awake.

When she heard Jack's voice, she felt herself go weak with relief.

'Where are you? I've been out of my mind with worry!' she blurted out, her hands gripping the phone so tightly her knuckles were white.

'Darling, I'm sorry about that. I tried to call, but I couldn't dial out.'

He sounded as pleased to hear her voice as she was to hear his.

Now she knew he was all right, relief gave way to anger.

'Have you any idea what I've been going through? You didn't tell me where you were going, just that you'd be back — and then you didn't turn up! Can you imagine the kind of things that have been going through my mind?'

'Yes, I can,' he said softly. 'And if there had been any way I could have come back, I would have. I don't suppose it's any consolation to know I haven't stopped thinking about you all night,' he added softly.

Margaret fell silent, not trusting herself to speak. Now she was thinking straight, she realised something very important must have stopped him coming back to the hotel — back to her.

'Are you all right?' Her voice was more steady now.

'I'm fine. I'm with Gordon.'

She gasped in surprise.

'I can't leave him alone right now,' Jack went on before she could say anything. 'Could you come here? Could you drive Luis's car if I gave you directions?'

'Gordon Robinson?' She frowned. 'But I thought . . . '

'You don't have to come — I'd understand if you'd rather not.'

'Of course I will! I've come too far to back out now. Besides, I want to see you . . . '

'Good girl.' There was a sigh of relief. 'Ask Luis for a map. Tell him to show you the best way to La Casa de Valle. Got that? La Casa de Valle'

'I will. Jack . . . ' She drew in her breath. She longed to tell him how much she cared, how much she loved him. In the end, though, all she could manage was a rather weak, 'Take care, won't you?'

'You too, darling,' he replied gruffly. 'Drive carefully. I'll be watching out for you.'

She put down the phone. What was Jack doing with Gordon Robinson? And what did he mean, he couldn't leave him alone? Had he been hurt somehow?

She dressed quickly and combed her hair. There wasn't time for anything else.

'What about breakfast?' Luis said when she asked him for a map and directions.

'No time!' She smiled at his shocked expression. 'It's all right, I'll have something later. Now — where do I go?'

When he'd finished speaking to Margaret, Jack put down the phone. He was smiling. It always gave him a lift to speak to her — even if she was angry with him!

He turned to Gordon and his smile faded. He was slumped in an armchair, sleeping heavily.

Despite everything, Jack couldn't help feeling sorry for him. They had been friends once, good friends. Then money and greed had spoiled everything.

With a sigh, he lifted the receiver again and tapped out another number, one he knew off by heart.

It rang and rang and he was on the point of giving up, when he heard someone lift the receiver at the other end.

'Hello, it's Jack . . .'

An Awkward Situation

Back in England, Angie had just given her father the morning mail when she heard a car pull up outside. She glanced out the living room window.

'It's Bill.' She turned to her father. 'Oh, Dad, what are we going to tell him?'

'The truth.' He shrugged wearily. 'What else?'

His wife was still sleeping in the spare room. She'd hardly spoken to him today and now she had taken herself off for a long walk — on her own!

He felt so helpless. There was nothing he could do to ease her heartache. And so much of it had been caused by his deception, well-intentioned though it had been.

Bill came straight into the house, straight in to the living room.

'Well?' he demanded. 'Is there any

news? Has Margaret been in touch?'

Andrew got slowly to his feet.

'Bill, sit down. I'll try to explain what's been happening.'

As Bill sank into a chair, Angie muttered something about a cup of tea and escaped to the kitchen.

Bill looked up at Andrew, the man he had hoped would one day be his father-in-law.

'She's with Jack,' Andrew blurted out.

'I might have known!' Bill's voice was furious.

'The important thing is, she's all right,' Andrew went on, suspecting that Bill wasn't really listening.

Angie chose that moment to come in with a tray loaded with cups and a teapot. She looked anxiously at her father. It was obvious from his expression that Bill hadn't taken the news well.

'It won't be for much longer,' Andrew told him dismally. 'The police seem to know where they've gone. They were here yesterday asking all sorts of questions.'

'Maybe it's for the best!' the younger man commented angrily. 'I'll be glad when Stanton's locked up. He's caused nothing but trouble between Margaret and me. If it wasn't for him, we'd be engaged by now.'

Andrew paused long enough to give Angie a brief, reassuring smile, then turned back to Bill.

'I know how you're feeling,' he said gently. 'But think about it! If things had been right between you and Margaret, Jack Stanton wouldn't have made the slightest difference.'

'Dad!' Angie was shocked and made frantic faces at him to stop, but Andrew shook his head. He knew the torment Margaret had been going through, torn between two men.

The whole family would have liked to see her happily married to Bill — they were all fond of him — but it was time they started to see things from her point of view.

'If it hadn't been Jack Stanton,' he went on, 'it would have been someone else. You've known each other since you were kids. I'm sure you love each other, but are you in love?'

Bill went very pale. Seeing how upset he was, Angie went to his side.

'Don't take any notice! Dad's upset. He doesn't know what he's saying . . . Dad, Margaret would be horrified if she knew what you were saying.'

There was a terrible silence. Then Bill began to speak.

'I think Margaret would probably agree with all you've said. Maybe I've just been too blind — or too stupid — to see what was happening.'

He sounded so bitter that Andrew's heart went out to him. But he didn't regret telling him how it was . . .

'Where's Ben?' Angie suddenly thought of her brother. 'Didn't he come home with you?'

Bill looked sheepish.

'I left him behind. I didn't say anything about Margaret. There was an auction and . . . Well, if it did turn out to be nothing to worry about, I didn't want to miss . . . There was a complete set of smithy tools . . . I couldn't risk missing them . . . '

He sounded defensive. He realised how much he'd said — without meaning to — about his true feelings for Margaret.

He *did* love her, he *did* care — but not passionately, single-mindedly and wholeheartedly. And now he realised Margaret felt the same . . .

Angie poured the tea and handed him a cup.

'Thanks.' He smiled sadly, no longer angry or defensive, just resigned. 'I wonder where Margaret is right now? I hope she's OK.'

He took no more than a couple of sips before putting the cup down and standing up.

'If it's all the same to you, I'll be getting back. Ben was nervous about the auction . . . '

Andrew walked with him to the door.

He felt embarrassed and sorry but, at the same time, glad this part was all over.

He was just saying goodbye when Jenny walked briskly around the corner and turned up the path.

There was something different about her, he noticed. She looked calmer, as if she had come to a decision after a period of doubt . . .

He patted Bill's shoulder, then went into the house leaving the other two outside.

'You're not leaving already?' Jenny reached up to kiss Bill's cheek. 'Won't you stay and have some dinner with us?'

'No thanks.' He shook his head. 'There's nothing I can do here and I've left Ben to cope on his own.'

She sighed. 'You know then?'

'About Margaret running off to Jack Stanton? Yes, I know about it. I would have thought . . . ' He broke off.

'Yes?' Jenny prompted, putting her hand gently on his arm.

'I would have thought she could have trusted me,' he blurted out.

'Maybe she was hoping to be back before any of us realised she'd gone. She wouldn't have wanted to hurt you . . .'

She felt so sorry for Bill. She had known him since he was a boy; he was almost like one of the family!

He sighed. 'Maybe.'

Jenny kissed his cheek again and gave him a motherly hug.

'Give my love to Ben. And drive carefully, won't you?'

She watched him go. The usual bounce in his step was missing. It seemed such a shame when everything else was going so well for him.

I hope Margaret realises what she's doing, she thought crossly, letting a nice man like that slip through her fingers . . .

There was a touch on her shoulder. Andrew had come to stand beside her.

'That poor lad,' she said crossly. 'What's Margaret thinking of?'

'It's sad, I know . . . but I think he and Margaret have simply outgrown each other. If he really loved her, there's no way Jack Stanton would have been able to come between them. I'd never let anyone do that with me and you!'

She turned to face him. He was right. If they had been in the same situation, Andrew would have moved heaven and earth to find her. But, then, she would never have rushed off after another man . . .

'Oh, Andrew, I just wish she would come home,' she whispered.

He opened his arms, offering reconciliation, yet fearing rejection.

Jenny took a step towards him, then she was in his arms, hugging him.

'Welcome back.' His voice was choked with emotion. 'I've missed you.'

'I've missed you, too,' she admitted. 'Will you help me move my stuff out of the spare room?'

'I can't think of anything I'd rather do right now!' he sighed happily.

The Truth Emerges

It was incredibly hot, even with the car windows open. Margaret was relieved when she saw the big black iron gates of the villa loom ahead of her and saw the name on the gatepost: La Casa De Valle. It was the right place.

She parked the car and climbed out. She could see the house beyond the gates — a large, sprawling building with a red roof.

There was an electronic whirr and she looked up to see a security camera on top of the gatepost wheeling round to point at her. Then the gates began to swing slowly open.

She stepped through and they moved again to close with an audible click behind her. She shivered. There was something sinister in the sound.

'Margaret!'

Jack's voice was a shout as a door in

the villa was flung open and he rushed out to greet her. She watched him run towards her but then he stopped just a few feet away.

'Hello!' He looked sheepish. 'Are you still mad at me?'

His boyish grin made him look irresistible and it was all she could do not to laugh out loud and throw herself into his arms. But that would make it too easy for him.

'Yes, I am!' she said with mock severity, but it was no use. Next moment she was in his arms and looking up into his face.

'I'm so glad to see you,' she murmured.

He held her tight, as if they had been parted for weeks, not hours. Then he bowed his head and kissed her and her heart soared.

'I've been watching out for you,' he told her, raising his head. 'I hated the idea of you driving here on your own, but I didn't dare leave him . . . '

'Him'? Gordon, presumably.

'What's going on, Jack?'

Slipping his arm around her waist, he led her into the villa. Large swirling ceiling fans kept the atmosphere cool and she drew in her breath as she looked around. Everything was beautiful — and expensive.

'Through here,' Jack directed.

Together they went into a large, airy living room, beautifully furnished in traditional Spanish style.

The first thing she saw was the man from the petrol station, slumped in a chair, and she stopped abruptly.

Jack put a reassuring hand on her arm.

'Gordon — I believe you've met Margaret?'

Margaret eyed the other man. He was no longer cool and immaculate and arrogant. Now he was unshaven and untidy — and vaguely pathetic. She despised him for what he had done to Jack, but then, if he hadn't, she and Jack might never have got round to admitting their true feelings for each other.

She suddenly realised why he had seemed familiar. He had been to the office once or twice with Jack, always smartly dressed, dynamic — and in a tearing hurry.

Now, he looked as if he had slept in his clothes. In fact, he still looked half asleep. He hadn't acknowledged her at all.

She moved closer to Jack, feeling nervous.

'Sit down. I'll get you something cool to drink,' he told her, giving her a reassuring wink.

Margaret sank into a chair, never taking her eyes off Gordon.

'He's near breaking point,' Jack whispered as he handed her a tall glass of orange juice chinking with ice. 'When I got here last night, he'd been drinking. That's why I had to stay with him. He's only just woken up.'

There was genuine sympathy and some affection in his voice.

'You sound sorry for him,' Margaret said. 'How can you? After what he's done to you?'

Gordon heard her. He raised his head and looked at Jack.

'I had to. It was you or me. I couldn't bear to lose all I'd worked for . . .'

He broke off. Jack said nothing.

'I know you think I only care about making money,' Gordon went on. 'But I love Susannah. More than anything. And I thought she would leave me if I couldn't give her the things she wanted. They offered me a lifeline and I grabbed it with both hands. If I'd known where it would end . . .'

Margaret shook her head slightly. She couldn't believe that all this had happened, all this misery, simply because Gordon was afraid of losing his wife!

'You don't know her very well,' Jack was saying angrily, obviously meaning Susannah.

'It's over, isn't it?' Gordon murmured, and he sounded so full of despair that even Margaret couldn't help feeling sorry for him.

'It's not over until I hand that disk

— and the password — to the police,' Jack reminded him.

'Do you really think I could go on living with myself knowing you were in prison?' Gordon protested.

Margaret went to Jack's side, squeezing his arm. She wanted him to know she was there, right beside him, whatever happened.

With a sigh, Gordon got to his feet, stumbling slightly.

'Let's get this over with . . . '

Jack and Margaret exchanged looks and followed him into a small study where he sat down at a desk and switched on the computer there.

Then he got up and offered Margaret his chair.

'It's all yours.'

Jack glanced at Margaret as she sat down, then took the disk from his pocket. He held it in his hand for a moment or two before inserting it into the disk drive.

'You'll have to give me the password, Gordon,' he prompted.

'Suzie.' Gordon's voice cracked on a wry laugh. 'The password is Suzie.'

Margaret keyed it in and almost at once there appeared on the screen in front of her a list of all the files on the disk.

She began to open them, one at a time. There was so much information there that she would take hours to go through it all, but she had seen enough to know that this was all they needed.

'Names, dates, places!' she cried enthusiastically. 'Jack, it's all here — everything you need to prove you're innocent!'

'And that I'm guilty,' Gordon put in bitterly.

Jack was standing behind Margaret, his hand warm on her shoulder, staring at the screen, and as he took in the information, she could feel the tension seeping out of him.

They were so engrossed, they didn't notice Gordon pouring himself a large drink. He took a sip and shuddered.

'I despise myself.' He spoke almost to

himself. 'For doing that to a friend. But at least none of that heavy stuff had anything to do with me.'

Jack looked up, but Gordon wouldn't meet his eyes, just went on talking.

'As soon as I realised the kind of people I was mixed up with, I tried to get out. But they blackmailed me with what I'd already done. I don't suppose it matters now.'

'I believe you, Gordon.' Jack went to him and took the drink out of his hand. 'You don't need that. Why don't you go and have a shower, then go to bed for a few hours? I'll be here when you wake up. We've a lot more talking to do.'

After the faintest hesitation, Gordon nodded.

'Will he be all right?' Margaret asked when he'd gone.

Jack stared after him, deep in thought.

'Gordon? Oh, yes. He's one of life's survivors.'

She looked quizzically at him.

'Why don't you hate him?'

He shrugged. 'He's still my friend. And he was desperate. In a way I feel *I* let *him* down by not being there to help . . . '

He heaved a sigh, then took her hand, holding it tightly as his eyes looked into hers.

'I'd never have got here without you. Whenever things looked hopeless, I'd think of you — trusting me, waiting for me — and I'd know I couldn't give up.'

* * *

Some time later, Jack checked that Gordon was asleep, then suggested they go out into the garden.

The breeze blowing down from the mountain was warm, but fresh and clean, and Margaret was filled with a sense of well-being. She was here, with Jack, and she couldn't think of any-where in the world she would rather be.

They were walking hand in hand when Jack stopped suddenly and turned her to face him.

'I wouldn't blame you if you never trusted me again . . . ' he began, then stopped, cupping her face in his hands. 'But I don't want to make another decision without you . . . ever. I want you to be a partner in the business.'

'Partner?' Was that all he wanted her for?

'You don't have to do that,' she said, somewhat tartly.

'Yes, I do. You deserve it. Without you, there wouldn't *be* a business.'

She pulled away, but he pulled her back again.

'That's not all. Not just the business, I mean. I want us to be partners . . . what I'm trying to say, and making a complete hash of it is — well, I'm trying to ask you to marry me.'

Margaret's eyes widened. It wasn't the most romantic marriage proposal — but it was the most welcome.

She couldn't speak. She simply gazed up at him.

'I love you!' He was beginning to sound rather frantic. 'I've loved you since — oh, I can't even remember! I never did anything about it because there was always Bill but . . . What do you say, darling? Please say you'll marry me!'

She didn't have to think about it; she already knew what her answer would be.

'Oh, yes,' she breathed happily. 'Yes, darling, yes.'

★ ★ ★

Much later, back in the villa, they found Gordon downstairs, fully awake and sober.

'What happens now?' he asked.

'Margaret and I will go home tomorrow — with the disk — and start getting this mess sorted out.' Jack reached for her hand and their eyes met. 'Then we have a wedding to arrange.'

'Congratulations,' Gordon said mechanically, then he shook his head, and held out his hand to Jack. 'I'm sorry. I mean it — congratulations. I hope you'll be very happy. As happy as . . . '

'There's someone at the gate!' Margaret interrupted, as the warning bell sounded somewhere in the villa.

Gordon looked nervous. The police? Or his 'business partners'?

'Don't worry.' Jack sounded remarkably calm. 'I'll see to it.'

Gordon and Margaret stayed in the villa and anxiously waited. Neither spoke.

When they heard him calling for Gordon, they both scrambled to their feet and rushed outside.

Margaret watched as a car drove in through the gates and parked in front of the villa. The door opened — and Susannah got out.

She pushed past Jack without even seeming to notice him and ran straight into Gordon's arms.

'Oh, darling,' she cried. 'Why didn't you tell me?'

'What are you doing here?' Gordon thrust her away. 'Are you mad, Jack?

Didn't you tell her . . . '

'Jack told me everything!' There were tears on her cheeks. 'I don't care if you haven't a penny! I don't care about anything except you and me and making our marriage work. We can do it!'

'You don't know what you're saying,' Gordon protested.

'Yes, I do! For once in my life, I know exactly what I'm saying and doing. I love you, Gordon. Don't send me away — please.'

'Come here.' Gordon's voice was barely a whisper as he embraced her.

'I don't think we're needed here any more,' Jack murmured, taking Margaret's hand, and, together, they slipped quietly away.

A Final Decision

Margaret twiddled nervously with the catch of her bag as Bill approached the quiet corner table in the local pub and put their drinks down. They had hardly spoken two words since they'd met half an hour earlier.

'Thanks,' she said.

'I hear Stanton's been officially cleared,' Bill said as he sat down, and his voice was cool.

She nodded. It was all over at last. And it even looked as though Gordon, who was co-operating fully with the police, was going to be dealt with leniently. She was glad about that, for Susannah's sake.

The silence stretched on, then they both spoke at once.

'I want to . . . '

'We have to . . . '

They both stopped, embarrassed, ill at ease.

Margaret insisted that Bill should say what he had to say first.

'All right.' He sighed resignedly. 'I asked you this once before and you couldn't give me an answer. Do you mind if I ask you again?'

'Go ahead.'

She knew in her heart what his questions would be — and what her answer would have to be.

'Are you in love with Jack Stanton?'

'I'm sorry,' she said honestly. 'I wasn't sure before, but now . . . Yes, I'm in love with him.'

He looked bewildered and confused, as if it was the last thing he had expected to hear. Obviously he had been nursing some faint hope . . . and now she had shattered his dreams once and for all.

She reached out to him, wanting to offer some comfort, but he moved away.

'I'd better be going.' He sounded distracted, as if he was trying to keep his emotions under control. 'I've a lot to do at the museum.'

'Bill . . . ' She couldn't bear to see him like this, knowing it was all her fault. But what else could she have said?

'Don't.' He put up his hands, warding her off. Then he drank his drink down in one gulp and left the pub.

Margaret watched him go, tears burning her eyes.

★ ★ ★

The Harris family were gathered together for the celebration meal Mrs Harris had spent hours preparing. Jack was there, too, as was his mother and his godmother, Edith. Even Louise, Jack's secretary, had been invited.

They were celebrating the end of a nightmare. Jack had been completely exonerated and things were finally getting back to normal.

There was also Margaret's promotion, to partner, to celebrate. And Louise's, who was now her personal assistant.

The conversation was bouncing back and forth, lively and cheerful, when the doorbell rang.

'I'll see to it.' Andrew got to his feet. 'It's probably just a double glazing salesman or someone!'

However, when he returned a few moments later, he looked grim as he caught his daughter's eye.

'It's Bill,' he announced.

What did he want? Margaret hadn't seen him since their last disastrous meeting in the pub. In fact, he seemed to have been avoiding her, only coming to the house to see Ben when he knew she wouldn't be there.

Now he stepped into the room, looking embarrassed to intrude on what was obviously a party.

'I'm sorry. I didn't realise . . . I didn't mean to interrupt anything.'

His eyes met Margaret's for a moment before he looked away. At the same time, she noted how nice he looked, all dressed up, and she wondered if perhaps he should have been invited to this celebration. After all, he had been involved in the trouble too.

He glanced at Ben.

'I just came to ask you, Ben, if you could come in a little earlier tomorrow?'

'Sure.' Ben grinned eagerly. 'Any particular reason?'

'I've got someone coming to look the place over. But besides that, he's looking for a bright young graduate to join his organisation and I thought you . . . '

'You mean it? Wow! That's terrific! Thanks, Bill.'

'You realise I'm cutting off my own nose here?' Bill sounded more relaxed. 'I'm probably going to lose my right-hand man!' He started towards the door. 'Well, that was all I came to say, so . . . '

'Won't you stay and eat with us, Bill?' Mrs Harris offered impulsively.

'I'd love to, but — ' he glanced at his watch ' — I'm on my way somewhere.'

'A drink then?' Mr Harris suggested.

'No — really. I didn't intend to interrupt your evening.' He said it without any bitterness and even managed a smile for Margaret before saying goodbye.

In the silence that followed, Margaret rose from the table.

'I . . . I'll just see him out.'

Bill grinned as she caught up with him in the hall.

'I know my way out well enough by now. I should do. This has been like a second home to me for so long. But thanks anyway.'

At the door he turned to face her.

'I'm glad things worked out for Jack. I really mean that. I just hope he realises how special you are.'

'Oh, Bill . . . '

'Got to go,' he said cheerfully and gave her a brief peck on the cheek. 'Have fun.'

She watched as he hurried away to his car. There was someone sitting in the passenger seat, she noticed. A young woman — whose face lit up as Bill got into the car beside her.

She felt her heart lift. She had done the right thing, she knew she had, and now it looked as though Bill might be beginning to realise it too.

She was still smiling happily when she returned to the dining room.

As she sat down, Jack reached under the table for her hand.

'Is everything all right?' he asked quietly and she gave him an almost imperceptible nod. Everything was fine. Never better.

'Shall we . . . ?' he murmured, and again there was that almost imperceptible nod.

He cleared his throat noisily and stood up.

'There's something Margaret and I want to tell you,' he announced, and an expectant hush fell over the company gathered round the table.

Andrew stopped in the middle of refilling the glasses and glanced at his wife. She smiled at him, her eyes sparkling.

'We're going back to Spain,' Jack went on. 'We'll be staying with Luis and his family.'

'Spain?' Jenny Harris echoed. 'For a holiday?'

Margaret giggled and Jack grinned.

'Stop teasing!' Margaret whispered to him.

'Not for a holiday. For our honeymoon!' Jack laughed gleefully. 'We're getting married.'

There followed a moment of silence. The news wasn't entirely unexpected, and yet . . . But then suddenly everyone began to talk at once.

'I want to be bridesmaid!' Ben joked.

'Only if I can be best man,' Barbara Stanton put in.

'That's wonderful news,' Mrs Harris declared, and she realised she really meant it.

She got up to embrace first Margaret, then Jack.

Andrew got on with filling the glasses and then he lifted his and beamed at all of them.

'To Jack and Margaret!'

'Jack and Margaret!' everyone chorused.

Because it was traditional at such occasions, and because there was nothing in the world she would rather do, Margaret kissed Jack, her future husband, the man she had never doubted and knew she never would . . .

The man she loved . . .

THE END